I Never Dreamed You'd Leave In Summer

Peter

Thank you so much for

Robert Lashley

your support

Robert Lashley

DEMERSAL PUBLISHING

Cover illustration by Spur Lowe Gardens.

Cover design by Zach Wise.

Author photo by David Blair.

Published with permission by Demersal Publishing, LLC.

Printed in the United States of America.

Identifiers:

ISBN 9798988180906 (paperback) | 9798988180913 (ebook)

Library of Congress Control Number: 2023937081

DEMERSAL PUBLISHING, LLC

www.demersalpublishing.com

PO Box 575
Tacoma, WA 98401

To My Closest Friends:

Sarah, Anna, Annie Lynn, Matt, Chris,

Mary Jane, Marie, Conn, and Allie:

I hope you know how much I love you.

To My Editors:

Marena: for your old-school work ethic and believing in me.

The 11th Street Editing Company: I hope I did right by y'all.

Conn Buckley: You helped me fly and land this plane. We both grew in this, and I am grateful for how you helped me.

To Matty and Carrie: For first taking chances on me.

To Christina: For continuing to do so.

To My Ancestors:

Mama, Big Mama, Aunt Helen, Eulalah, Virginia.

Uncle Moe, Herman, and Milton. Uncle Mike, Uncle Robert,

and Den Mama Tracy, Lisa, Aunt Pat,

and the babies we have lost on these streets in the last few years:

I will never forget you.

•••

I'm not Grendel, I'm worse than that nigga. You shouldn't lift a fucking finger to help me in anything again.

It was big-minded of you to talk to the family on my behalf. I know I'm not your favorite nigga in the world. After our seminar last summer, I overheard you say to Dr. Everett that I achieved cheap grace, that our first seminars weren't fruitful, that I was skating by standing behind him and not truly addressing what I had done. I didn't address you with anything other than a head nod afterward because of that, I thought you were just a hater who was jealous and scheming to kick me out of his house and be the center young man again. I thought I had it made, dawg. I was on the stage with Aunt Estelle and Kyle when Dr. Everett said he was getting all these equity deals done and having these public ceremonies with Black people getting paid. I had served my time in Juvie, did the men's classes with y'all online, and was doing good in school, so I didn't like your ass. I didn't understand why you were coming at me with all this extra accountability and discipline shit you was talking about. But then today happened.

To keep it real with you, I knew today was going to come. I just didn't know it was going to be at the school. I had the voices I showed today in my head since Juvie but I'd train myself to Dr. Everett's videos. When I came to the house, we'd have exercises where I would chant his High-Class Hotep chants. *I will destroy the Crip inside me by being a Nubian warrior. I will quell all weakness and vulnerability in my mind. I will be a king and an alpha in my dealings in a racist society.* I could will myself past the guilt I had with the chants, and I did them through the almost all-White neighborhood and the almost all-White school. Whenever my voices would bubble, I tried to will myself with thoughts about Africa, my inner Black kingship, and the strength of our people.

But I wasn't in the almost all-White school anymore. I was in this place that looked like a series of big-ass castles, with cathedral halls and neat-ass lawns. I was all-round all these different looking people than the ones I was used to, and I didn't want to alpha on them and fight them like in the professor's exercises. I looked over to the manufactured lake and saw James and Darren, some boys I knew from prep, and I thought I could hang with them, shoot the shit, and escape before orientation. They were laying in the cut in the back from everybody talking a bunch of cool shit. And I wanted to lay in the cut in the back talking cool shit. And I was right with them for a while, being big and confident, talking big shit, and hollering at girls.

Then, right before we were supposed to go, I saw Judith, a girl who used to live four blocks down the street from the family house. I didn't use to think of her and pull some high school big-talking shit when we were going to prep, but when I saw she was in college and was wearing different clothes, I decided to come up and holler at her. I tried to step to her with some smooth game, but she told me to leave her the fuck alone, and when I asked why she said, "Because you called me Big-Booty Jewdy for most of my high school life."

"I'm sorry about that," I said. "I'm going to college and am starting to mature–"

"Is that supposed to fix everything?"

"But I've changed."

"I don't care, man."

"But I've been doing these classes and changing my behavior."

"It's not my job to validate you, Albert."

As the crowd started forming around us, she got in my face and just read me, "I wish you well. I don't want anything bad to happen in your life. But I have scars because of how mean you were to me. And 'hey girl, you're looking good now' is an example of your changing? I lost weight and have a fucked up perception of my body because you called me Big-Booty Jewdy until I was a senior. Eight months ago. You haven't referenced my heritage and my size for eight months. And now you want a medal."

People came around me when she walked away. Before she left, Judith turned around, "when you learn something about my culture other than a cruel, punny reference to my ass, you may come unto the phrase, 'Go with God, but Go.' I wish you no ill will. But I'm still paying for you."

I'm still paying for you. I couldn't get the sentence out of my head. I had spent years telling myself I was different, that I was fixed. That the years of Hotep chants, my placement into prep, and me being a college man washed the trap robber away. That I wasn't the monster anymore. Yet here was this decent person telling me I was a monster, and here I was spitting game to random ladies a second before being a lighter version of a monster. Maybe I just got lucky.

Until that day, every time I'd think of what I did, I'd hear Dr. Everett and Aunt Estelle say that I wasn't that person because I wasn't in that environment. But I am; I got to hurt people, and good things happen to me. I saw that at the school, and it started to kill me, because I saw myself. Just the same nigga with a few years of pity compliments and privilege. I spent three years not looking at me, not looking at what I had done, and just thinking that it was all my environment. But then I showed I was just the same nigga, only with more of a leg up.

I sat in the Pierce Hall dining room for another orientation shift just fucking dazed, hearing and seeing everything I had done over and over in my head. After a while, James and Darren came up to me and started talking cash shit about being rejected.

"You got turned down, playa," said James, popping down on the table bench in front of me.

"Fucking pussy. You're gonna have to be the pill man if you want to hang with us," Darren said behind him.

And they kept talking about how I couldn't pull the deal off, how I was such a wimp and how if I was going to hang with them, I needed to bring pills and shit. They just kept talking about pills and shit. Just kept talking and talking and talking... And every time they kept talking,

I heard more voices and got sicker and sicker; because when they started talking about pills and girls, I thought of Big Thomas. I thought of all the body chores I had to do for him, and I just lost my mind.

I know you both told me to get Thomas out my head and not use that as an excuse for the shit I did, so I tried to do our exercises again. I tried to do all the mental empowerment exercises you showed me in that Les Brown seminar. *Excuses are lies wrapped in reasoning. Excuses are lies wrapped in reasoning. Excuses are lies wrapped in reasoning.* But the voices couldn't stop. They just couldn't stop. And James and Darren couldn't stop. And I just broke to the point when you saw me talking all this crazy shit about what Big Thomas used to do to me; how I don't want to be like Big Thomas, how I don't want to be like James and Darren more, how I don't want to be here, and how I wasn't shit and they wasn't shit either. That's when they jumped on me and started screaming that I would rat on them. They just kept punching me and punching me, and I started screaming. After that, you broke it off, and that's when I started running and talking all out of my head.

Professor, I am such a fucking fake. All the shit I did being a runner and robbing old ladies, and for what cost? To end up in this nice-ass neighborhood? With my aunt all nice and sweet and forgiving and shit? I don't deserve any of it. I shoulda just done my time. You, Aunt Estelle, and Dr. Everett put so much into me, and what did I do to earn it? All of the counseling and the talk of trying to reclaim my young innocence and being a Black man in the streets and getting these chances to better my life, and I didn't think about the chances those old ladies I robbed didn't have.

Just leave me to the shelter, dawg. After all you tried to do for me in your conscious men's class. After all Aunt Estelle did for me sticking her neck out to get me out of Juvie. After all Dr. Everett and the family did in allowing me in the house and helping me live a good middle-class life these past three years. And this is how I repay y'all. I'm back at the shelter now; all these niggas who used to rob me and I used to rob are looking at me as meat, and I ain't got nothing to say them. I don't want to take up any more space. I'm good with these streets.

I'm okay with being homeless right now. I do my reading and writing and have my computer time at the library. I don't deserve anything else. I'm not Grendel, professor, I'm worse than that nigga.

• • •

I appreciate Dr. Everett and Aunt Estelle coming down to the shelter parking lot and I'm sorry I caused so much trouble between them. Please tell them I'm not mad at them, I just freaked out because of the tension of their arguing. Dr. Everett wanted me to take a series of T.D. Jakes' seminars on manhood and toughness, and Aunt Estelle said that we should go back to the studies we did when I was in Juvie and they escalated like I've never seen them before. I felt so sick that I did this. This didn't happen before me, professor.

I don't want to return to school because I don't deserve the fifty-'leventh chance. I know the basement floor of the shelter is dingy and has rats, but I can cry without the tweaker ex-sailors and ex-Crips fucking me up. I know I did that trap shit, but I'm a frail motherfucker, and thugs can smell that on me. But please don't cry for me, professor. I am a demonic knucklehead for what I did. My momma disowned me for my street shit before she died. I go to the library and then hustle to the center to get my two meals and a cot; I can't fuck up anything now.

The streets seem like the place I deserve. The lamps flutter and morph into various shades of reddish off-white, distorting the reality of what I see, never giving me a second of peace. The colors on the hill that came from these various shades only light enough to leave shadows, unseen avenues, and pockets of darkness to keep you on your toes for every crinkled leaf, far-away scream, busted carburetor, and any other not-quite-right sound that would give an active imagination an inkling of peril. This is the world I deserve, sir. This is the world I deserve.

Please tell Aunt Estelle that I won't bother her anymore. I don't want my bullshit to reflect on her. The Everetts are a notable and important Black family. You are a good brother, dawg, and a good counselor. And if they did nothing but help you come up from the block when your momma and your auntie died, they did more in a day than I will ever do in my life.

You'd always complain I never kept it real with you, so I will say this now. Do you want to know my most cowardly act that day? I didn't think of my mother. I was so wrapped up in my own shit, I didn't think of my mama or the lake or losing her. I remember the last time I saw my mother. Big Thomas promised not to fuck with me in the booty if I robbed a White lady down the street. He said he'd give me a chance to sell some weight and not be a runner and not have my body messed with. And for that chance, I grabbed a lady's purse. But what was so fucking stupid was that I did it right in front of a cop's house. I remember being arraigned and looking for my mother like I usually did, preparing a sad, "streets is hard" rap about how I was set up. I was thinking of the society's stories you hate so much to convince her that my life struggles were the only reason I'd mess with an old lady like that. I was prepping it like the ones I prepped before and always thought she would believe.

But she was there this time and not looking at me, and when I said "Mama, Mama," she hissed. As the judge read my charges and I went to my usual rap, she would mumble and look at her big-ass *Beowulf* book. When I saw her in the last few months and was deep in that stickup life, I noticed she'd read the book obsessively. I used to read with her as a boy, but by the time I was thirteen I was so scared of the heads of the neighborhood runners and what the fuck they would do to me if I showed I was a nerd and shit. So when people asked me about the book my momma was reading, I would say "the book is called booger wolf, like your momma."

But that afternoon, she didn't nod when I looked at her. She was talking to herself and yelling at the book in a tone I'd never seen her have. When the judge told me I was gonna spend my teenage years in Juvie and if I saw him afterward it would be my adult years running out of chances, my mother slammed the book down and tried to put her arms around the cops saying, "burn him. He has given me horns. The monster has given me horns. I have loved the monster and he has given me horns."

I didn't know shit about Grendel then, but I knew I had lost my mother. After she died, I read *Grendel* in Juvie, and wanted to slit my fucking wrists. Grendel's mama was ride-or-die for her son, but Grendel didn't curse what he taught her. He may have been a thug, but he didn't curse her.

• • •

Professor Thompson

I have so much gratitude for you, Dr. Everett and Aunt Estelle. I almost can't put words to it. There is a lightness in my heart that wasn't there. Y'all coming together to give such a detailed plan for my life is the best thing to ever happen to me. You created the raft and the plan that will make me a good man. Your love for me made me believe in God and I don't even like God.

I promise I will adhere to y'all's therapy rules and do everything at Mrs. Eulalah's beauty shop you want me to go to. I understand you want to help me level up in my self-examination. I will dedicate myself to being honest about how I turned into an abusive young man. I will work on my life choices and dedicate myself to never be that nigga again. Someday, I'm gonna write a memoir and gonna save hood niggas who had to come up just like me, who fell and turned out wrong for a while. Then, I'm gonna do all your writing exercises and observe people, observe history, and take notes on myself. After that, I promise to go deep into myself and take your notes and our group talks seriously. I've been doing those yoga breathing techniques like you told me to, and have been running more errands with Aunt Estelle. It feels good that she trusts me, but I don't want to get that comfortable feeling which leads me to take her for granted like I took my mama for granted.

I struggle with your last order, I'm not gonna bullshit you. You told me to remember my mother talking or trying to teach me a lesson, and I've been trying. I've been trying so hard. I would see her on the bus telling me about the plotless myopia of John Williams, the broken bondage between Sula and Nel, leaning in my dreams, and moving in thought to break my own curse to see if I could learn something I couldn't seven years ago. But every time I come close, every time I break the mold of the stories in my brain, I hear her scream those final words and snap out of it in a hell sweat.

I'm gonna do good for you and the family, and maybe then I can hear her again.

• • •

Professor Thompson.

I had a great first day at the salon, and Mrs. Eulalah laid down the law with my ass, "There will be no umpteen little chances with me, nigga. I'm only doing this because it worked with Andre when Estelle sent him. But Andre didn't do time roughing up women like you. I like Dr. Everett nowhere near the way your family and internet niggas like Dr. Everett. But I love Andre, and I'm doing him and Estelle a favor. Don't embarrass them and make me regret it."

Sitting in her main chair on the west side of the room, I was distracted by the colorful combs and picks sticking out of the neon blue jar labeled "Barbicide." I kept looking at them in front of a mirror covered in beauty product stickers and thinking they looked like weird garnishes in a rapper's drink, but snapped back when she surveyed her shop with her index finger, "you have one and many jobs here, Albert. They are to do whatever the fuck the chair and the customers tell you to do. Some trucks come in the parking lot every day to serve breakfast sandwiches. Some trucks come in here to serve fish sandwiches. Some trucks coming here to serve green vegan shit. Your job is to get whatever breakfast sandwich, fish sandwich, or vegan shit the people who sit in these chairs want. After that, your job is to do whatever the heads of these chairs say. I am the first chair; the second chair is Nona, the third chair is Aisha, and the fourth chair is Macalester. I will not be here at times because I have to oversee business at my shops downtown, the city limits, and on the east side. In that duration, Nona, who is what?"

"The second chair,"

"Correct! Nona, who is the second chair, will be your God as much as I am now. Nona's gift with hair, customers, and creams has kept this shop afloat. Nona and Aisha run a book club here on Thursdays, and your job is to get them all the food and wine they need to get right. When Nona needs to go to the Lowe's in University Place or South Tacoma to get art, you will escort her to make sure men do not corner or harass. If you give any guff about Lowe's or her choices for art posters, I will cut the bacon off your back. I'm going to let you know that Nona used to be in a rap group. If you have any, or discover any aspirations to be an MC or make it in rap, do not ask her a single question about that rap group, or I will cut the bacon off your back. The third chair, which is who?" she leaned in for my answer.

"Aisha, her daughter."

"Correct again! Aisha, who is a genius at making highlights with Skittles colors work. Aisha will also be with us after shift doing her studies, special hair weave orders, and working on marketing for me because I don't know what the hell to do with these young people and the goddamn internet. If you flirt with her the way you flirted with that Jewish girl (or flirt with her in any way), I will cut the bacon off your back. The fourth chair, who is?"

"Mclester," I said as I scanned the Black hairstyle guidebooks on the magazine table next to the couch.

"Wrong!" she smacked her hand on the leather chair rest, snapping me back to attention, "phrase it with me. Mac-a-Lester."

"Mac-a-Lester," I sounded out the syllables as she did.

"One more time. Mac-a-Lester."

"Mac-a-Lester"

She gave the slightest nod of approval, "Macalester isn't as good with hair, but she is brilliant at doing feet and weaves that my Black ass is too old to understand. When you are with her, you will help her with the boxes that come in with the product that helps keep this salon afloat. Your first job in the morning will be to iron her caftans. You will also escort her when she goes to get plant ornaments and pots and make sure they are clean every morning. Macalester walks our customers to the bus stop just in case men corner or harass. You will help her in this and walk women to the bus stop or their cars if they ask to. If you give her any guff about why or that the men are just 'being nice', I will cut the bacon off your back. Macalester used to be a man but came into herself and her journey. You know this now, and if you call her Lester–"

"You will cut the bacon off my back."

"Look at you learning!" she said, raising a flask of Crown Royal to me. "Your job here is not to burden them for a second. You are in a space to heal, make our lives easier, and pay your cosmic debt to society. You are not here to do whatever you want and fish for compliments. If you want to do whatever you want and fish for compliments, there are countless environments that will indulge you as such. You, however, are in mine."

Everything went well because I let everybody know it was my first day. I was transparent that I didn't know shit, and I wasn't going to have an attitude about anything. They were very merciful toward me.

Mrs. Eulalah let me home early to work on my writing lessons for you both, so I decided to write you from the Starbucks across the street from the shop. The outside table on the back side is my quiet place to get work done. I do my lessons here for you and Dr. Everett and do my best to hear my mother. I am trying so much to hear my mother, professor.

Y'all both want my first lesson to be me being clear and direct about my origin story, something that doesn't involve me blaming my father, the Man, or the streets for any of my actions. Here is my best attempt at that in writing.

I was born at the Hillside Terrace Housing Projects when they used to be the projects and not bougie-ass condominiums. My mother's name was Vonetta Robinson, and she and Aunt Estelle were sisters in everything but blood. They were among that wave of Black folks to come to Nisqually Prep school after University Place lifted their codes and lawsuits against the government because their football team was losing. My momma and Estelle were hardcore book nerds as tight as two toes in a sock. They lived at Mrs. Ethylene's, Mrs. Eulalah's grandmother's project, because their fathers were church deacons who only understood the language of an ass kicking.

I learned about them only in subtext, that they were best friends who had come from the bottom projects of Moncks Corner, South Carolina, that their wives were loyal behind their men when they had become deacons in the church, and that that church had some sort of Black Conservative right-wing hustle tied to a motherfucker named Oscar Micheaux. That hustle had enough to get them out of the projects and live with their husbands in small houses by Division Street, but they were so Pentecostal that they didn't go out the house, and my mother and Aunt Estelle were all but on the streets by the time when they were thirteen.

You know all about how Mrs. Eulalah came up here from the Third Ward in Houston, how she served as a nurse and how she pooled and hustled her money when her left toe was shot off. She met them, my momma, and Aunt Estelle, by the time they were running the streets and took them in to work at the shop. When they got to college, they drifted because my father went into a punk band that got some play and did a tour, but they fucked up their chance when my father got into PCP. I am not blaming her health problems for my shit: like many people did that drug and lived, and many people don't have sons that become coward-ass derelicts who prey on people trying to make it. I know she had health problems, but that wasn't why she died. I'm pretty sure my being a fuck up contributed more to that.

I can't tell you that there was a direct before/after with Big Thomas. I remember my mama being my world like so many other little boys. I just knew that outside the world was shooting after shooting after shooting. And beating after beating after beating. And being so scared of that world. And every little vulnerability and sensitivity I had being grounds for an ass whupping. And there was Big Thomas offering me protection, food, and candy. If I just did what he told me. If I just ran his bags to cars that came.

And after I said yes, there was no pain. Then Thomas took his protection away. More was needed to for me to be safe. Packages, then touch-the-body games, then feeling that my body wasn't mine anymore and feeling so fucking angry at the fucking world. And thinking that anyone in my neighborhood on the block had no right to be happy. Anybody with a smile. Anybody who looked innocent. Anybody who looked like they still had something I had, I'd fuck up. Men or women. Then Thomas wanted to see me beat and rob that church lady. Then that White lady, and Juvie, losing my mama, and looking at the mirror and seeing a nigga with horns look back. Every time I look in the fucking mirror, professor.

I cry when I see what a life we could have, professor. She could have been healed, happy, and writing if I had got my shit together when you had initially tried to talk about books with me. I would get into dysfunctional debates with you, spewing some shit about how reading the classics wasn't tied to the struggle and what a Hotep OG legally hustling was supposed to be. I was full of shit, professor: I didn't read literature because it reminded me of how much my mother loved it, and how much I fucked her over. In the suburbs and going to bookstores and art galleries with Aunt Estelle, I can see my good memories of her and the chances we could have had if I wasn't such a fucknigga.

My aunt talked to me about honoring my mother by honoring her books, and my momma gave me so many, professor. I know she made her money on disability and working under the table at Goodwill, but she was at her best when she was writing and trying to process her blues. She wanted to write a great masterpiece about a sister getting out when she was back in the hood, so I knew about William Faulkner and Toni Morrison when niggas were learning their ABCs.

I hope y'all can help me come back to the person I used to be. I GET why Aunt Estelle never gave up on me. In making sure I live well, she is trying to make sure her connection with my momma will last, and I was too stupid to understand that until now. I hope to prove myself worthy of that investment and faith someday. I hope to prove myself redeemable someday.

• • •

Professor Thompson

I appreciate everybody in the family for helping me find the best of myself. Running errands for the local church shut-ins has given me perspective about my own ego and conduct. I know I skated on using institutional circumstances to explain my mess-ups, but I'm gonna get right, I promise.

Also, your social justice videos with Dr. Everett are inspiring. I am fully committed, professor. I know that by speaking truth to power I can use my mess-ups to be a force for social justice and help other people not make my mistakes. I'm gonna be the best scholar I can be for social justice and protesting for all these Black folks getting gunned down by police.

It has been an honor sitting behind y'all in symposiums, conferences, and speeches listening to you tell it to the Man, and to see you get businessmen and creatives paid is an honor. Y'all have taught me that this pain I feel, this pain about the loss of the right of Black people to assemble peacefully, the Ferguson Police Department following the COINTELPRO playbook to the letter; children getting shot at with rubber bullets at night, and having White racist motherfuckers calling them thugs in the morning, is real. We are going to have to fight it. And the way I fight it is to be conscious, go to the library, and train to be activists like you.

I'm aware I got a good thing at Nisqually. Dr. Everett has got me a free ride on his tenure plan, and I'm going to get my books and syllabi early to show that I mean business. I know he isn't my father, and he's told me as such. I know my coming into his house was stressful because of the attention Aunt Estelle pays to me, and his son Kyle acting up. But I'm gonna work to heal everyone, professor. Maybe we can work together like a family? I know the professor complaining that Kyle was an alright assistant to him until he got into his "punk goth phase." Well, every time I get him to talk outside of pouting he says nothing is good enough for him, that he can never be enough of a Black warrior for him. I try with Kyle, professor: I tell him Eulalah and the shop doesn't hate him but he just can't talk to Black elders like his gamer friends. And I'm gonna keep trying.

My goal is to be a scholar and writer like y'all. To have a Victorian house on high like Dr. Everett and come down to the community to help people come up. I'm gonna bide my time and earn this legal hustle. I love my room in the basement; I have space, and the patio is hella dope. It's so much better than the dorms, to be honest. All I got to do is work at Mrs. Eulalah's beauty shop to have spending change. That, and be on garden duty at the house. Aunt Estelle is having me go over Gloria Naylor this week, and is telling me all these stories about how she and my momma used to debate about the intricately constructed Black worlds in *Linden Hills* and *Bailey's Cafe*.

I sit in my spot at Starbucks before and after work and try to hear her monologues about how she would search for geraniums to get her mind right. I used to walk with her when I was a baby, but stopped when I became a street associate. I try to hear her when I am sitting to write you, and trying to hear her when I am with Aunt Estelle. I am trying so hard to hear her again, professor.

• • •

I promise to not be wrapped in myself so much and focus on other people in my writings. My self-focus spilled into the shop the other day. Mrs. Eulalah and I are okay, and I promise never to be all spacey in my thoughts like I was yesterday at the shop. I was going good until then, and she offered me some needed correction. She offered me needed correction on a lot of things, and I've been thinking about them ever since.

I got so wrapped up talking about Dr. Everett's *The School* today that I forgot my place at the shop. I have read his articles and his videos about racism, equity, and what the White man puts us through, but I had never read his autobiographical novel until now. Wow, sir. Wow! I didn't know the trauma Dr. Everett went through to become a social justice scholar, and it was beautiful that he documented his struggle through art and dealt with racism in all-White schools. I dig what he says in his videos about Black manhood and the pain we brothers go through, but his art, professor, is something else. He and you were like I was as a kid, but y'all had more courage than me because y'all didn't punk out and be a runner. Y'all took that sacrifice to be successful; getting up 4:30 every morning, taking the bus to Nisqually Prep, and y'all went there when it was worse for Black folks. Especially

Dr. Everett: I mean to have to get a lawyer and go through all these backlash White motherfuckers protesting (and to detail it like that).

The problem with all this art talk from me was that it made me slow in getting the orders for everybody, and she had every right to cuss me out, "nigga, stop talking about that goddamn book in my goddamn shop. That nigga's been living on that goddamn book for thirty goddamn years. And don't think that part about him leaving that Jewish girl had any meaning. They went back and forth with each other for ten years. I stuck my neck out for the nigga when he was a wounded little boy going to that school and did all I could for his ass until he snatched Estelle at nineteen and told me at the wedding that I get to be subservient for the 'New Movement.' And you need to get his milquetoast anti-Jew shit out your head, boy. Acting like niggas can differentiate White folks like that."

As the entire shop stopped, she sunk into her first chair and took a deep breath, "that was one beautiful thing about your mother, Albert. She had her principles. She couldn't give away ice water in hell when she was in one of them moods, but she had her principles. She wasn't about that anti-Jew shit. She was talking about all the forward things I see on social media thirty years before social media. Put in my head to accept Macalester, yes she did. A year after your mama drowned herself, she comes in here, 6'2", 220, wearing camouflage and green dollar store rouge. And though I didn't know shit about her specificities, I knew she was climbing the rough side of the fucking mountain. She came in here looking for a job and a chance to do something better, and I had to give her that if I was worth my salt. Your mother taught me that. Your mother said, you need to accept her. If you are to become whole, you will respect the best of your mother in this building."

I thank Aunt Estelle and Mrs. Eulalah for teaching me to be conscious of others. If my momma could see me become a writer in the spirit world, she would forgive me, forgive me on that day when I see her on the other side. I'm gonna do good in school and keep on the weekly personal life skills classes she makes for me.

Also, I appreciate you talking me into joining the Hilltop men's group you took over from Dr. Everett. I know you wanted me to be there for a couple of years, but to help me when my life was on the line because of my fuck-ups was big of you. I know Dr. Everett is like your father, and our relationships are different. You did none of the bullshit I did, and for you to reach out to save me because of my bullshit, I see what you do, man. Taking hours at the school, running classes on the block, yet still having time to run errands for the sick and shut-in. You and Dr. Everett are a team of what Black men would be, local and national. I'm gonna make you proud of me, I promise.

• • •

Professor,

I've been doing better with my chores at the salon, so much so that I've been granted special privileges! Macalester allows me to come with her to the docks where she gets bootleg weaves for cheap-ass prices. I help her get the boxes, and we eat at Dairy Queen afterward. Not the one downtown, the one across the street from the Amtrak station. I dig that joint; it's open 24 hours for graveyard shift factory workers and rent-a-cops. The restaurant is clean, the food is cheap, and the people seem pleasant, so it's a dope place for me to write while she reads.

"I'm gonna give you a little bit of the game, young nigga," she said to me yesterday as we finished up burgers, "you doin' okay, but you need to stop saying 'I'm sorry' so goddamn much. You say it every nine sentences. You interrupt conversations of people you don't know. People start to think you aren't really sorry, just searching for absolution so that you can move on with your life. If you are really sorry about your actions, show it with different actions. Not the sad boy production you lapse into sometimes. You doin' a lot, and that's good, but work on that. Can't tell you anything different."

We throw our trash out, and I see Macalester wave to the manager, then go over and hold his hand. I couldn't help myself, I let out an, "Ooh."

"Nigga are you twelve?" she responded.

"I'm not hating."

"Mind your business."

"Look, I'm not gonna get in front of your game. I get why we get our weaves around here. You can spit game at whoever–"

"First of all, young nigga," she grabbed my shoulder so hard I couldn't move, "we get our weaves out here because there's too many niggas around the neighborhood Black beauty stores that would see me as meat. That is one of the crucial reasons I bring your Black ass around so that I could have some sort of reinforcements so that Black men won't feel the need to instigate shit. Do you understand? I'll feed you all the burgers you want, but nigga, you better know the assignment if you gonna ride with me."

She took a deep breath and leaned on her van. "His name is Les. And yes, Mr. 'whoever,' he's still a he. We were on the same football team in Puyallup. We were on the O-line back then, and we were pretty good. Les and Lester. The Twin Tackling L's for the opposition. We were scrawny little boys then who didn't know our elbows from our asses about gender dynamics, but we liked each other, felt good, and felt dishing and taking pain was a way of processing. Judith Butler could have gone to town on our asses.

"One night, we overslept in our special place. We would have a special place, Albert, the old tackle machine equipment room. Because our football team was so bad, nobody would go in, and we made it our love nest. We put in a mattress and had lube, oils, and everything. We had spent all this time building a DIY dream world. We had made love in the same spot we did the first time. I dreamed we were dancers in France, and I bought him this big ol' apartment. In that dream, I remember I had surprised him. I had bought him this beautiful cottage, and we were riding on a horse-drawn carriage. I had blindfolded him, and just as I was about to open the blindfold. I get a kick in the forehead that spins me to my side. I open my eyes and see this big man kicking and kicking me with this big steel boot. It was our defensive coordinator. He hit me in my head, in my face, and all over my body. I look up, and I see Les freezing. I rolled over my body, which hurt me cause I got a thorn in one of my open rib wounds, grabbed my clothes, and ran screaming."

Macalester patted herself down, then shook a Backwood out of a soft pack she found.

"I had nowhere to go," she lit the cigarette and took a long pull. "The only reason I was in Nisqually was because I was living with my grandma at the senior home on the outskirts. She wanted me to pray the gay away with her and live in University Place with more of a conservative Christian influence. It was okay because I was basically living by myself in my room and could pull the wool over her, but when I got back to the senior center, I wasn't allowed at the gate. I had been kicked off the football team, and they said I had hurt the team. I had nowhere to go."

The bell on the Dairy Queen door chimed, and Macalester pointed at Les coming out of the Dairy Queen, meekly nodding to her as she blew him a kiss.

"What am I supposed to see?" I asked.

"Use your street associate powers, young nigga." I eyed him over and saw Les had junkie pimples, then looked back toward Macalester. "The first time I saw him again I was at the food bank line, and he was driving down 6th Avenue with his family going to a psycho revival meeting at the dome, run by one of those life centers that want to pray the gay away. He looked at me from the backseat for a split second with this stupid yearning look, and I just hissed at him. I thought he should have defended me. I felt he shouldn't have frozen. I thought he chose White instead of gay. And every time we crossed paths, that's what I'd do because that's all I saw."

She took a final drag and stomped out the half-finished smoke out expertly with the heel of her '96 Jordans.

"Then ten years later, I was running errands for the Unitarian Rainbow Center, working that same foodbank line, and I hissed at him again. And he flinched like I used to do when I saw my daddy. His family had kicked his ass to the curb just as much as mine did, only gradually, and he didn't have Eulalah to give him a life. The only thing he had was the pipe, which he still struggles with."

"Big time," I said, smirking.

"Nigga this ain't a T.I. movie," she grabbed me by my Nisqually jersey. "I pay him respect when he's dopesick. I give him money. I do all these goddamn things because when he was tender with me, he gave me a sense of who I wanted to be. He gave me a sense that I could live with it, that there was a world and places hidden within this world that were bigger than my mean-ass family. I can't put a price on that, Albert. So if he can't get well, I give him some money to get right, to not suffer."

Les got in the van and gave me a side-eye.

"We're already late for book club. That's the story. Never come at me with some macho shit about my personal life again, or I'll beat the reformed trap boy out of you."

• • •

Professor Thompson

Sula! Oh my God! I reread it! I'mma cry like a motherfucker. The friendship between the two, Nel and her, from day-one in the mud (or to be precise, the ironically titled "Bottom"). How they go separate ways, how Sula breaks Nel's heart by taking her man. But how Nel grieves her when Sula dies and the Bottom convulses in joy. I know why Aunt Estelle has so many copies of that book now.

Also, I went to the last orientation today and I didn't fuck up. I'm still processing, but I didn't fuck up, When Mrs. Eulalah's Lincoln zoomed past the Nisqually Prep bus stop, I felt a spirit, as if I was taking steps to make my chariot come up. Normally, I'm not a church nigga, I used to go just for the food, but I learned some shit. And I felt that shit today. I felt it the entire day, professor, instead of nerves. Even Dr. Everett told me he was proud of me. He took me out for breakfast and gave me compliments about qualifying to go to Nisqually. It was the first time we had a morning together. We went to get the breakfast special at the fish house at Titlow Park, and he told me I could be a good role model for Kyle, who wants to be a gang banger now. I know Dr. Everett is a hardass who has problems feeling emotion, but I'm glad he's finally trying with me.

I was sitting in Mrs. Eulalah's car with Aunt Estelle doing all the processing techniques you and the fam were talking about (breathing, not being a follower, thinking of other people). I thought of my momma and what she thought of when she was here. Did she have a sense of wonder about all this? Or did she have more complex feelings because she wasn't a lucky criminal and a fuck up like me?

"Before we go to the school, get me a pulled pork sandwich from Jackie on the second grill," said Mrs. Eulalah, interrupting me, pointing to the cooking spread Nisqually had prepared for the students. "And I need you to tell her to come back to the shop and resume my Scrabble butt whuppings."

"I don't feel I deserve to be here," I said.

"Shut your behind up and focus on the future." Mrs. Eulalah got out of the car and pointed to the school, "You got a truckload of work too and I's to dot and T's to cross before you can do it. Sobbing about your fuckups isn't gonna get anything that you need to do done right now."

"And you should be here," said Aunt Estelle as she straightened out my jacket "You took advantage of the chances we gave you, and you got the grades. Now go take advantage of this one."

We get out of the car and walk across the gravel track to the cookout. We blend into all the families, and everything seems a blur of emotional goodbyes and smiles. Walking a block past the grass, we move to a fork in a road that leads to a red square on one side and the dorms on the other, and walked into the admin building. After that I felt numb going from room to room to get my new responsibilities and papers. Insurance? Meal plans? Bus plans? Computer room plans? Then people in these big-ass halls telling me of the things I must know to be a responsible student?

I was still kind of dazed when I was done with everything three hours later and I saw Mrs. Eulalah, Aunt Estelle and Aisha at the top-floor cafeteria. They were working on the hair of two freshmen girls that looked like twins. Aisha was wearing a UW sweatshirt and putting different colors and strands together on a table before placing them into packets.

"Go get us five ice mochas from their machine in the kitchen while we finish this," Mrs. Eulalah said to me while I was coming toward them and through the cafeteria to check-in.

I walked back through the cafeteria slow, weaving through the empty tables, then lingered to look at all the old, gorgeous Catholic Jesus art on the school walls, and out the stained glass windows overlooking the water.

I got their orders and returned to them twisting and putting pins on the young women's parts. I put the coffee down as Eulalah and Estelle put scarves over the twin's heads. While they were waiting for the parts to hold, I went back again and got a burger and a Cherry Coke for myself. After a few minutes of looking out at the water while eating, I saw them take the scarves off to show identical, tight-cropped hairdos.

"Voila," said Eulalah, holding up a compact mirror.

"Do I still have it, Tamika?" Estelle asked.

"This got me through the army," Eulalah said to Jamika. "Wasn't no place to get styled in a station in Libya."

"Thank you, Ma'am," said the girls in unison, then giggled at their echo.

"And take these with you," Aisha said, passing her the weave bags with her card in it.

"Next time, don't be pulling a girls hair when you make the parts like you did today," said Eulalah.

"I had to speed it up. We only had three hours."

"Well then establish a time when you can do it longer. Go back to the dorm and talk to them. Go, I said. Establish a base here."

After they nodded, said thanks again, and left. Eulalah looked at the back of the twins' heads and turned to look at me. "Your mother used to have that, but she wanted a part that made her look like Rosalind Cash on *A Different World.* Would just fuss at me when I had to put four pins to just hold it, but I told her she wanted her hair suspended in-air like that, I would have to work."

"Oh, when we saw Rosalind Cash in high school she went nuts. Found all her videos in the library. Got us into Shakespeare when she played Goneril in *King Lear.*

"Netta's gender-bending Lear would scare niggas."

"You ain't never lied. Nothing would scare a man wanting some tail off by getting bug-eyed and yelling 'eyes, I'd use them so / That heaven's vaults should / Crack.' "

"I loved it so much," said Mrs. Eulalah, "you entertained my ass as I closed shop."

"Good lord, your mother wanted to be a playwright then. In high school, we would read plays to each other on the bus, and she would put her whole body into a performance. Just immerse herself in characters with her energy; Blanche DuBois, Lear, Lena Younger. Every time I was tired of busing or wanted to quit or wanted to go away because my daddy didn't love me anymore, she would be there and..."

And after that, they stopped. Aunt Estelle draped her arm over Mrs. Eulalah, who helped her to a chair. "Best life I could possibly have," Estelle told herself.

"Just try not to think about it, baby," Eulalah said.

"She just ran off that road we were on and kept on running," she walked to the window overlooking the manufactured lake, dirt path, pavement road, and water, pointing to each with her index finger, "Just. Kept. Running off. The road."

"I know, baby, I know," Eulalah went toward her and I followed.

"Just. Kept. Running off. The Road.

"Best life I could possibly have, Eulalah."

"I know, baby"

"I get this boy over here," she waggled a finger at me, "when he is an inch out the pen, and get him back to test into his grade and out of Juvenile Hall, and the only time he takes off after he's out is when another Black man's involved."

"I know, baby."

"Netta is still gone, my actual child sings a slave narrative when I tell him to do something, and my husband's freaking the fuck out about his ex-woman, who's the head of the humanities department now, talking all this shit about changing his teaching style trying to get back at her."

"A nigga can't get a White woman out his system."

"Ever since she got that job, he's fighting with her like the times we just met, and it makes me wonder, who the fuck did I choose?"

"What y'all talking about?" I asked.

"Nigga shut your behind up and stay out our business," Mrs. Eulalah snapped at me, "you already got a Candyland life after sticking up women, getting a free ride to college and shit, don't get into our business and the bullshit we have to deal with. You already have a good ride and damn near everything. Let us deal, boy. Not everything is about you."

Just then Mrs. Estelle looked at her, and both women took a deep breath. "If you want to do good for us, then do good in school, run errands for the women in the shop, and try and be a good man every day. Or at least try to be a better one. This is bigger than you," said Mrs. Eulalah, "today is bigger than you."

Next time we talk in person, professor, you got to tell me what they are talking about. You want me to write what I see, I'm writing what I'm seeing. And it's starting not to jibe with what y'all been telling me. Maybe you can help him with this. Maybe you can get him off his focus on his ex-woman and onto the focus on getting people paid and making the system better for everyone. I'll be the first to tell you that we all fall. Let me be the first to tell you that we are too important to each other to stay down. I have faith in us. Let's talk about it.

• • •

First, the good news: I heard my mama today! I heard her for the first time! Sometimes I try and break down, which is something I can't do around the shop. But I was reading James Baldwin like you were telling me to do, and I got to the point to the church scene in *Go Tell It on the Mountain*, and I could hear her clear as fuck! I could hear her at the Community College bus stop talking to me about Baldwin fusing the language of the King James Bible with Henry James' prefaces, and rhetorical gravitas of the African American storefront preacher. Right there I looked up gravitas. *Noun, dignity, seriousness, or solemnity of manner.* I used to love that about Dr. Everett 'til he got obsessive about his ex-wife.

I found out about a lot of shit in my life yesterday, and I'm processing it. You told me to listen to people and write what I find, and I'm doing that. But I got a lot of new questions about our conscious men's class.

I've been working extra hours at Mrs. Eulalah's doing corner store errands for the customers, and I pulled a whole shift for Women's Day. It was a little after seven, I had took the last creams out of the boxes, put them on the tables behind their chairs, and took out my notepad to take down whatever order she and her new customer wanted.

"Albert, before you go and get me a coffee cream and– what you want, Glenda?"

"Chocolate coffee blast," said the young woman in the chair, "gotta be at the orientation party at the mall tonight."

"You heard that?" Eulalah asked me while combing her hair into five separate rows, twisting each part upward into the middle of each row. "But before you get them, get the box from the basement closet that says 1987."

"Word," I said, "you gonna tell me about African Queens and Black beauty. Dope."

"That's your warning," she said deceptively sweetly to me while finishing the fifth part. "Talk about a woman's hair choice in my shop again and I'mma knock your fucking teeth out."

"I'm sorry."

"Get the box, then our orders, baby."

I went downstairs, got the box and handed it to her without saying a word and went to get the orders. I came back to see Eulalah and Glenda sitting together, looking at the wigs. "Your mama taught me this," Eulalah said to me, looking up. "I can't help but feel certain feelings about her. She was the most goddamn difficult employee I ever had. Especially when she got sick and needed side work money. Everything about her chafed against what made me who the fuck I am. Y'all talk so much shit about how hard your streets were? Y'all couldn't have lasted a week in the Galveston I grew up in. The metal storage room in the back where we have the chairs and the grill? Put a bad sink in, and it's where my ass grew up. So I struggle with this Evergreen thug shit, and I struggled with your mother, especially in the end when she would come in here all haggard and wanting to talk me down about every fucking thing.

"But when your momma was right, she and Estelle gave me something of the mind and the imagination that nobody else would. When I'd have them close for me, and they would talk to me like they wanted my opinion about books, that I was capable of talking about books. So I kept up with them and vested so much of myself, so they could succeed."

Mrs. Eulalah lined up a dozen wigs on the magazine table for Mrs. Glenda to see, smoothing each one out as she put it down.

"When she got on SSI, she'd come here and argue with me and be a cynic with me about every fucking thing in the sky, and we broke. I would be on her to get a job and get on with life after your daddy had his breakdown. I'd be on her hard to do something, to at least do something with the literature. And I'm sorry she lost her marbles. I'm so sorry she jumped into the water. I know you feel guilty, but I have my feelings too. Maybe that's why I gave your ignorant ass a chance."

I looked to my left, and I saw Aunt Estelle listening in the couch. I wondered how long she was there and how much she had heard. Mrs. Eulalah looked at Glenda, and presented her with the choices from the bottom of the box, "Which brown or black one you want?"

"The black one on the end right," the sister said.

She put it on the top of her head, "there you go, baby. They can't do nothing to you in Nordstrom with the Anita Baker wig on. It's tight cropped, passes their 'non-ghetto sophistication test', won't cost you much, and the White boys who you don't want to fuck with won't fuck with you."

Glenda admired her new look in the mirror while Mrs. Eulalah put together a bag with hair caps and wig pins. Mrs. Eulalah handed her the bag, and Glenda, looking pleased, gave over a small wad of twenties, which Mrs. Eulalah stuck in her smock pocket without counting.

At the front of the door, the two women hugged. As she pulled away Glenda asked, "is Nona okay?"

"She's doing good, Glenda," she replied.

"I'm sorry for blaming her for the paper going down. The horrorcore rap news happened so fast along with Rodney's suicide."

"I know, baby."

"I was young and I just spiraled. Since she was in the group, I looked for someone to blame. I'm sorry I yelled at her every time our paths crossed."

"I know, baby. Someday, I hope you can say it to her."

"I hope so too," Glenda paused a moment at the door, "I'm gonna keep getting better. Thank you for letting me back in."

"I believe you. And you're welcome, baby."

"One more thing," her standing in the open doorway let the night's chill into the shop, "what about Terrence?"

"That's a hard question, baby," Mrs. Eulalah put her hands on her hips, "I read his articles for the Peninsula Papers. He makes a little money writing Black shit for them. He's still a conservative but not good at it because of the drinking."

"Do you think Sarah would approve?"

"We can talk about that another time. Best of luck at Nordstrom, baby. And come back and tell me everything about it."

"Who is she?" my stupid ass asked Mrs. Eulalah as Glenda closed the door.

"How many times do I got to tell you? *Stay. Outta. Black. Women's. Bidness, nigga.*"

After Glenda left we didn't say anything for hours, we just put the console back on and looked at old *Comic View* clips on YouTube. It was a little after 11p.m., four hours after the beauty shop closed, and an hour after the last of stores in the strip mall shut down. Lights came down slowly in all the shops while we were watching, and the high-beam-white sign of the Lowe's across the street turned black. Inside the shop's walls it was dark, save a lamp over the waiting couches where I was sitting with her and Aunt Estelle.

"Should we go?" I asked.

"I told your mama to get away from that band life as fast as she could," Mrs. Eulalah said me, "I don't try to hate your daddy per se, but the shit comes out. He thought he was gonna make it with a punk record? A punk-funk opera? I know she didn't get along with Everett, but rebel that much? We were so tight. She was the closest to me in my forty years at my shop. The grants that cover our overhead? That keep our prices low? She was the one who set that blueprint up. She sought the grants and made herself a grant writer for me. *At sixteen, Albert.* But when..."

Eulalah put her thumb and index finger on her eyes, then took an almost empty pint of Crown Royal out of her purse and poured it in her empty coffee cup. "I shouldn'ta told her to shut the fuck up and suck it up with Scott. She was never the same. I could deal with the blowout hair and the suit jackets. But that band? And Angel Dust? And fighting over almost everything. It still tears my stomach up. I can't get the voices out of my head. I run through every fight, breakdown, every time I could have stopped the escalation by agreeing to disagree, every time I could have let go of what she messed up and tended to her for who she was at the time. I know she didn't fully come back from that sherm shit, but I should have been more patient. I struggle with soft, baby. But I have days where I look in the mirror, and it just kills me." She took a slug from the cup and winced slightly from the straight liquor.

"No, it is my fault," I said. "I drove her there. I was the one who took what she taught me and ended up slinging rock and robbing old ladies and shit."

"You just have to pay it forward with your effort in school, baby," said Mrs. Eulalah.

Right then, the words came out of my mouth, "how was my momma like?"

Aunt Estelle put her hands together and looked at me, "she was the nexus of my fucking universe in Hillside Terrace. I wouldn't have dealt with everything if it wasn't for her. I wouldn't have dealt with all the trap houses. I wouldn't have dealt with the catcalling, and I damn sure wouldn't have dealt with the busing to the suburbs. Mrs. Eulalah grabbed us, and that was our chance. And I held on and grabbed to her, and set my life with my all-but-sister and closest friend in the world — your mother. We would do everything together. We went to the movies. We were bused to the same school together. We would get our breakfast from the fish fry in the morning; your mother and I would sit in the back of the 27 bus and try to hide our orange drinks. Your mother would eat peanut butter and honey sandwiches and go over my tables and my geology facts. We were the only people who wanted each other to succeed. And lord knows, she wanted me to succeed. Every time I was tired of busing or wanted to quit or go away because my daddy didn't love me, she would be there. And my momma and your grandmother would be there, God bless them. But for that goddamn jam funk band..." she trailed off and stared out the window.

"I'm not gonna lie to you," Mrs. Eulalah leaned forward to look me in the eye, "I'm gonna look you dead in the face and say this. Every time I try to like your daddy, I hate him, and every time I try to hate your daddy, I can't. He was a tall caramel boy who was big and dreamy like his father. A boy from Gig Harbor was the son of Black professionals who integrated Pay 'n Save's pharmacy department. They were nice people who sheltered him and wanted to give him the best, but he never had a bad day in his life. And didn't know how to deal with the damn White man. Just a goddamn dreamer. A sheltered-ass space cadet. He had some musical talent and had a band called Green Rainer Funk. But lord, the boy was spacy, dumb, and ambitious."

"Your daddy didn't want to make a record, Albert," said Aunt Estelle, "he wanted to make an *op-er-a*," she marked each syllable with her finger like a music conductor. "He did six songs with Green Rainer over the summer of our senior year at Prep and caught a break. Eleven-show gig with the Ohio Players. But halfway through, the money runs out, the dope runs out, and the Ohio Players quit. And your daddy can't quit sherm. And your momma was on that shit till she got pregnant with you. I found it on the same day. The same goddamn day."

"I tried to tell her to just work on her studies, to just focus on getting something tangible, but she fell for that boy," she exhaled deeply. "And she struggled with Everett. Good lord, she did."

"Look, you know I don't think Everett was a Jesus. And for the same damn reasons. Vonetta used to come and say he thought of me as a goddess and a queen but not as a human being. He used to come to the shop and tell me how much he's a fucking feminist but wants me to do all the wallpapering and the cooking and the bending, if I was gonna have a relationship with a good Black man," Aunt Estelle was on her feet now, pacing the room.

"Oh, I agreed with Netta," Mrs. Eulalah was tapping the last few drops into her cup, "I went so far as to go to his office with my second Sunday shit on and tell him to lay the fuck off my girls. But your momma had to think strategically, Albert. She just couldn't cuss at him like I cussed at him. She needed to just con him till the end of his 'improvisational Black humanities class' and go on her way–"

"But she wanted to fight-fight-fight the world," said Aunt Estelle, slumping in the second chair, "Hilltop, Everett, the school, everything in that damn universe. Even fuckin' sobriety."

"I remember her coming back and telling me she was in your daddy's band and I felt stabbed in the fucking gut." said Mrs. Eulalah, summoning Aunt Estelle's posture up with her left index finger, and grabbing a bottle of rosé with her right before sitting down in her first chair. "We fought so bitterly about that shit. And even more when they got a record deal and a tour, and she felt like a fucking prophet. She had shown her proverbial bossy momma wrong." She put a heavy pour in the cup before offering the bottle to Estelle.

"But I knew the tour was gonna be a shit show because even the White hipster local magazines ratted them out," said Aunt Estelle, grabbing the bottle. "And I knew it was over when she called me saying that he got on that shit and started talking about his mental spells; him being a vegetable and taking a dump in his pants." She gave a quick glance around for a cup, then took a swig when one wasn't in sight.

"I lent her the money to get a flight home, but she took a bus ticket," said Mrs. Eulalah, grabbing the bottle back and wiping the top of the bottle with her hand, topped herself off, and set it between them.

"I felt lost, Albert," Aunt Estelle said to me, "I was scared shitless that she was gone until nine days after the second year. She shows up in rags and a bump with you. And I'm like, 'girl, what's going on,' and she says she was gonna live on welfare and be a freelance writer, and there was nothing we could do about it. And I got scared. And I latched on to Everett."

"I didn't hate you for it," Mrs. Eulalah turned her knees toward Estelle, "I was mad at Everett because you were too young. But I didn't hate you."

"He paid attention. The Great Everett paid attention to me. He had high standards for my conduct! I was a project book nerd, and a great Black man of letters in the Pacific Northwest was giving me attention. And Vonetta wasn't, so I just drifted from her."

As the console clock flashed 12, she slumped deeper into the couch, leaned back and buried her head in her scarf. Mrs. Eulalah sat next to her, eyes starting to swim. "The thing that kills me. The thing that fucking kills me?" she scooped up the bottle and finished it, then turned on her side to face Mrs. Eulalah. "For all my anger at that boy. That stupid boy and band he thought could save the world through the jam funk. I knew he cared about her. He was a stupid little nineteen-year-old boy who ruined his fucking life. But he was kind to her. And goddamnit... goddamnit Eulalah, who is kind to me?" Aunt Estelle closed her eyes and wiped away a few stray tears. "I had to be a goddamn Lady Tolstoy of the streets and align myself with a local literary god-king to survive, a god-king who was interested in my too-young ass but was something, something stable to help me deal with

Nisqually because the stable person that kept me in Nisqually lost her mind. So I became the wife. So I fulfilled my obligation to the culture. Raised Kyle when Scott was in symposiums being 'Professor Everett.' Took Andre in when his momma died. Took you in when you couldn't stop fucking up. And I did it and did it and have done it for over twenty fucking years." She tried to set the bottle down off kilter and it clattered and rolled across the hard linoleum. The silence was stark when it stopped.

"I have moments where I just want that little thing they had. Just a moment where a brother just isn't taking. A moment where a brother is kind to me for a little bit. Just that little bit of kindness. Can I have just a little bit of kindness?"

So yeah, I've been learning a lot. We got a lot to talk about. And I got a lot to work on, kindness being the first thing. And I want to hear Dr. Everett's side of the story because if you want me to write what I know and what I see in my life, I'm gonna write some things he doesn't like.

• • •

Professor Thompson

We got to get Kyle into your men's group as fast as we fucking can because the shit just hit fucking hit the fan yesterday. I've always tried my best to help Kyle because I knew my position in the house and wanted to help the family. Because I was doing good, Eulalah agreed to have Kyle work with me when he came out of summer camp. But he came back as OG Fuck-Al-Uppagus with a bigger blaccent than a teen pop tenor. I could deal with sad goth Kyle and thought that the beauty shop would toughen him up, but this shit? This golf course gangsta shit? And asking me about shit he just saw on BET 'cause he thought I'd be an expert? I tried to tell the nigga to take advantage of his chances and respect his momma, but who am I to say "respect your momma" with all the motherfucking baggage I got?

Last night Dr. Everett sent him to Mrs. Eulalah's with me for their fight night, and he showed his whole ass. You know how Eulalah got sisters who don't go to church but still like the idea of Women's Day? She has her own version of Women's Day when pretty fighters are fighting. A big part of my job there is to flip chairs, bring out tables, and cater when the fish fry truck comes. Kyle was supposed to help me clean the chairs and get the tablecloths from the cleaners, but he spent most of the day not doing that. He started talking this shit about wanting me to take him to the sets and sling rocks, and I am begging him to shut the fuck up, especially in front of Mrs. Eulalah, who has picked bigger niggas than him out of her teeth. But he doesn't stop, just doesn't stop, and goes on incessantly about nobody giving him attention even when his grades are good. I try to tell him that his momma and daddy do love him they just don't want him to pout all the fucking time, but he pouts even more when I say that.

Five minutes before Eulalah comes back with the bird, I take time outside to beg him to act right. I tell him —no, I invite the nigga unannounced to you, I'm sorry— to come to your group so he could work out his alienation and loneliness issues talking to other brothers out of the suburbs, but he said he was scared of being bullied and that he was bullied so much. I try to sympathize, but there is only so much I can do, so much I can feel and process, and when Aunt Estelle comes, I just tell him to focus on the food and the sisters.

It was close to fight time, and we had everybody situated. Me and Mrs. Eulalah notice him not passing the food out so tell him to leave and convince her not to blow her stack as long as the nigga ain't in the room. We got everybody happy and having a good time and talking about their man Anthony Joshua. The sisters love Joshua because he's big, fine and has a left hook, so everything was right in Denmark, and they were prepared for their good-looking man to deliver an ass whupping. The ladies were fixated on Joshua coming in and the perm he had, and I was just focused on them because you know the tension of what happens before people fight, and I don't see Kyle come in and throw a chair at her big screen.

I jump him and haul on his ass. I know you probably saw Kyle and heard his version, but believe me, I had to do it. Even though it helped make the whole motherfucking scene a nuthouse. Sisters was trying to duck the broken chairs and refrain from the violence, and chairs and tables and food are turned. Macalester says she got to run out of the situation or she's put a cap in Kyle's ass. Aunt Estelle tries to tear me off him, and everybody says fuck him up. She screams "that's my son," and I stop. Mrs. Eulalah said, "well then, don't bring your son to this motherfucking beauty shop no more. You can bring Albert. Albert can work here. But don't bring that little golf course Crip to my motherfucking establishment."

"What did you just call my son?"

"You heard what I called your son. Your little privileged Piru done fucked up my big screen."

"Does that mean this thug has to kill him, and you fucking thugs just watch?" And when she said that, the entire block stopped. From broken chairs to beauty products to gas station wing orders 300 feet away, you could hear a chorus of shit falling to the ground from people's hands. I swear to God and four more niggas, professor, that was the most hush-over-Jerusalem moment in my entire life. Even Aunt Estelle knew she went too far because she started stammering, "I... I..."

"So we thugs, huh?"

"I... I..."

"We all a bunch of thugs, huh?"

"I... I... I didn't mean..."

"Every time your rich, woke man mistreat you, you got to come to me. And I'm a thug."

"I didn't mean it like that..."

"Every time the world don't go your way cuz you went off to a White suburb, you got to come to me... and I'm a thug."

"I didn't mean it."

"Go home."

"I'll make it right."

"Take your successful, sophisticated ass back to your successful, sophisticated neighborhood, and your successfully sophisticated, woke Black man, and leave us thugs alone."

In my mind, I can still see Estelle beside the passenger side of a car, looking at Eulalah and all the women in the shop. I can still see her face and complexion changing with the 7p.m. sun, still see her car right above the evergreens that marked the city limits for University Place, not sunset or twilight but the first sign that the day was losing its glow. I can still see Kyle in the backseat hyperventilating, then feeling something for him for a second until I see the passenger seat bob up and down and realize that he's kicking it.

"I'll make it right," Estelle said to the entire shop, "I'll help him make it right. I promise to help him make it right." She tried to say something else, then couldn't find the words and just closed the door. Mrs. Eulalah had me sleep on the couch in the basement because I understand I'm not Aunt Estelle's son. I'm not her son, professor.

• • •

I broke down. I hate myself for breaking down. I have to find a way to make my soul right with this undeserved life shit. I might not be a scholar like you and Dr. Everett, but I got to do something with my life.

It all started when I was having a day off, leaving the food court and seeing Mrs. Frazier at the bus stop. Mrs. Frazier was the first woman Big Thomas wanted me to beat. I didn't want to do it. I would usually just say: "this is a robbery," flash my gun, and people would submit, but Thomas wanted more now. And when I said no, he took me from behind in the dumpster behind Al Davies. So I went to the lady I used to rob when I was thirteen and hit her with her cane. I wasn't making any money selling rock, and I was too scared to rob motherfuckers bigger than me, so I saw her as easy money and beat her up and took her money like she was an ATM.

So, I saw her again, for the first time in years, and I got my wad of cash out. I hadn't seen her since forever, and I was doing good, and I was filled with this idea that I would be paying a karmic debt if I gave her what I stole from her.

I got off my bus and started to run to her, but I stopped and decided to move very slowly. I didn't want her to think I was robbing her again. Her bus was coming, and she was having someone help her.

"Mrs. Frazier, Mrs. Frazier," I said, but she couldn't hear me because she was so old. I get on the bus to look at her and take out my pockets. "Mrs. Frazier. Mrs. Frazier. I'm different now."

"Who are you, baby?" she squinted at me, searching my face for recognition.

"Mrs. Frazier, I'm–"

And as I was about to tell her, her caregiver interrupts, "where you get that money?"

"From my job at Mrs. Eulalah's, but I–"

"Then you keep that money, young man," she pushed my hand clutching the bills back toward me.

"No, no, I–"

"You make that money legal, baby?"

"Yes, ma'am, but–"

"Then, look at all the good you are doing with your life."

She turned around and started getting on the bus. I looked at myself and realized I was wearing these top-line Joe College threads: black slacks, brown sweater, Nisqually jacket, everything. I also realized that I had both had a growth spurt and lost 70 pounds. I turn around and see all these people looking at me. Some of them would have been frightened to see my face before, and now it felt like they were looking as if I was a prince. The caregiver told me, "you earned that money, you keep it. Spend it on a young lady," and turned and got on too. The people standing around nodded with agreement. As the rest of them got on, one patted me on the back and another actually tried to give me a $20. I was so scared and overwhelmed that I ran four whole miles to the beauty shop. I ran past the stop down the hill to South Tacoma Way, all the way to the bottom. I pushed myself, going through the business district and chop shops, consignment warehouses and car lots. I made all my motherfucking guilt into physical burning through my lunch and kick it into gear when I got to the Division Street strip mall where Mrs. Eulalah's was.

When I got there Nona was closing shop. I told her everything, and after I helped her in exchange for a minute of her time, she sat on her first chair, looked at me, and took out a smoke.

"Two truths stand, Albert. What Big Thomas did to you was horrible. But you will not become whole if you don't realize that you robbing those old ladies was nobody's fault but your own, and do what you can to make sure it doesn't happen to another woman."

"But why didn't they respond to me saying I was sorry?"

"Why didn't they? Albert, you put her hands on her. It's not her job to redeem you. It is your life actions, your understanding that you fall short of the glory of God and govern yourself accordingly so you can heal as much as you hurt on that corner. And I don't think you will do that by participating in one of Dr. Everett's 'High-Class Hotep' YouTube videos. Now, let me drive you home, it's late. Buy me a coffee tomorrow for the gas."

This is why I work at the shop, and still fuck with you and your men's group. Everybody tells me I'm some sort of hero, and I try to believe them, but I can't. I did too much dirt. I did some dirt, and I need to remember. I lost my mother's love and drove her to the grave. You, Estelle, and Mrs. Eulalah remind me that I am a lucky-ass nigga, and I have a debt to pay for what I have done. And I'll keep paying until the day I die. And I'm good with that.

• • •

Professor Thompson

Could you tell me what to do about yesterday's bullshit? Could you tell me what to even think about it? Because everything about it makes me want to quit everything we have ever done and tell all y'all to kick rocks. And I hate to put some bass in my voice when I talk to you, but you got some motherfucking questions to answer me. Has he done this shit before? All the shit you talk to my men's class about being conscious, respecting sisters, and respecting Black queens, you need to tell me if he's done this shit before; and if he has, why didn't you tell me before yesterday?

I don't know what the fuck I did wrong, and to be honest, I don't think I did. For all the game the professor talked about Black women being queens; the professor went apeshit because Aunt Estelle wasn't wallpapering and cooking when he wanted her to. We showed up late on Friday because the shop wanted to throw a party for my progress at school. They had put me through the charges because of my past, and they wanted to show their appreciation for making something of myself. People talked about my momma, the strives I made in my life and my future, and what I wanted to do, and I felt so happy.

And we just kept it going without thinking about it, professor. Mrs. Eulalah wanted to play cards, and Aunt Estelle sent text messages for them to go get Uber Eats, so we didn't think nothing of it.

We come in like we usually do during those days. I'm running errands for her, not thinking we did a fucking thing wrong, but from that moment, my reality fucking changes. Here he comes running down the steps screaming, "I'm sick of this. I'm fucking sick of this. I can't have peace and normalcy in my own fucking home. After all I've gone and all I've done for you, I can't get a fucking family dinner. Not at least one family dinner."

I didn't know what the professor was talking about. Most of the time, he's gone trying to build his equity program, and Kyle is in his room either whining about shit or playing a fucking video game. Yet today, today he wants to have a family dinner. And now?

"I told you to order Uber Eats," Aunt Estelle said, as stunned as I was.

"I didn't want to order Uber Eats. We hadn't had a family meal since Albert came here. I'm going through all this stress, and I can't have consistency and stability to go home to."

"We can have family dinner next week or even tomorrow. The women in the shop wanted to do something for Albert because of classes next week."

"Albert, Albert. Why don't you stop doing something for that Crip and start doing something for your motherfucking son."

"Brother, get over yourself," and Dr. Everett slapped her. I don't even think. I push him, and he throws me against the wall. "After all I've done for you. I gave you both the fucking world, and now that my world is fucking collapsing, you have smart mouths. My ex-wife is the head of the humanities department, and judging from the shit she is talking about my curriculum, I know that racist bitch wants me out of the fucking school. Kyle is running around in these streets. My life is going to fucking hell, and all you can do is give me fucking mouth. After all I have done for you, you give me your fucking mouth."

Professor, I went into a fucking zombie mode. When I saw Aunt Estelle busted up like that, with her eye swelled up; shit, I went into my nurse nigga mode like I was with the young boys that couldn't deal with Big Thomas. I went up to the kitchen and got a bag and a compress to curb the swelling. I had all these motherfucking thoughts in my head, but the first thing I had to do was get her swelling down. Dr. Everett stormed off to his room to do another one of those videos, talking about how he gave his all in his intersectional class, and he can't give anymore, and I'm trying not to fucking go insane. He couldn't stop shutting the fuck up about his "phony White bitch" ex-wife, and I'm suppressing my anger. And how did I not know this shit? What did you put me in for? Who is this fucking man that I decided to worship? All this shit about him being a feminist and Black women being goddesses, and this was gonna be a stable home of consciousness and sacrifice, and the nigga ends up hauling off hitting Aunt Estelle like that. That was when I started thinking about your ass. Did you see Aunt Estelle get hauled? You coming in acting like such a fucking monk and shit, dedicating your life to service in the Black community and helping young men get better. What about you, dawg? What's really real about you?

After a couple of hours where me and Aunt Estelle just sat together at the dining room table, Scott came back in the room with waterworks, "I can't apologize enough, I backslid from my glory and teachings as a conscious Black man. I have backslid badly from the lessons of my life. Hitting you was the worst mistake I ever made, and I let the White man and a karen beat me down. I let a karen break my spirit. I let a White woman get in the way of the happiness of our family."

He then goes to Aunt Estelle and grabs her hands, "like I said on our first date. Being with her was the worst mistake I ever made in my life. When I was with her, I wasn't the man I am now and the man you helped me be. That you helped make me be with all your work and strength. I was an Integrationist when I was with her. I didn't have my conscience about the world and about Israel and Palestine."

And I tune out with that shit because it's easier to tune out and nod when the nigga is talking about Israel. I'm looking at him and still thinking about what you might say and why you haven't said it to him. Like, "None of this is an excuse to knock your woman out. There is no excuse to knock any woman out." And then I look at her, overwhelmed and nodding, and remember what I did before I got to her. I see her stressed out of her mind and think, "if I protest, it will stress her out more." So, I just hung my head while they hugged.

We go upstairs and order Uber Eats, and I'm thinking, "Eat, go straight to bed, and get this day from hell behind me." Then MC Snuff-Al-Uppagus barges in, wearing something that cost more than two of my mama's disability checks. "Where the hell have you been, son," Dr. Everett asks him.

"Doing what I need to do to acquire my shit. Like my shit?" He's parading his mall drill outfit in front of him, his mother, and myself at the top of the stairs.

"Please, Jesus, just talk about something else," I said, "Uber Eats is coming."

"I want to talk about my shit. Do you like my shit?" he put his left hand in my face to show me his jewelry.

"How's school, man?" I ask him.

"I quit, Cuz."

"Quit? Have you lost your fucking mind?" for a second, Kyle drops his act and backs up a foot from her tone, just like I do.

"I'm gonna be a rapper," he said, putting his street face back on.

"Rapper? Your golf hood burger ass gonna be a rapper?" I snickered.

"Watch your mouth. This is my son. You are a guest in this house. Estelle, this wouldn't have happened if we didn't give this nigga chances."

"Yeah," Kyle puffed up.

"Lay off him, Scott," said Estelle. "Yes, he fell to a dark place at a young age. But look at him now. He gives me honor. He listens to me and abides by me. He learns from me."

"Fuck you," said Kyle.

"Fuck you. That's right. I have a son who tells me 'fuck you.' I can go into town with Albert, and people would look at him approvingly, and for a second, I could fake that he is my son, that I had someone I could be proud of, and people could be proud of me for. But no, no, I can't do that with Kyle. I can't chastise my child because I would have been a ghetto-ass woman if I did that, and I have to be the everyday University Place housewife. I have to raise a friend. And what did that get me?"

"You're never gonna love me–"

"Oh, come off it, nigga. You can't do a damn thing in a private school yet expect me to play a deferential role and wait on you hand over foot. You niggas expected me to play servant to your Nubian king and prince."

"Shut up bitch," Dr. Everett sneered.

When he said that, I hit him. I remember the rest in blocks. The table going over. Dr. Everett hitting me with a plate. Blood in my eye. Me being thrown down the stairs. And Kyle screaming, "you don't know me. You don't know my struggle. Yeah, I was sheltered! When I was a kid growing up, I saw all these Betty Crocker mothers with beautiful dispositions and wonderful attitudes and wondered why my mother couldn't be like that. Why couldn't you be a cool mom and get me the stuff that White kids had? All the other moms would go on vacations and ride cars and act cool and shit, and all my mom would do was sit in the kitchen and listen to NPR and read books and shit. And all my dad would do was chase bitches at the golf course. Everybody loves you. Everybody loves you street niggas. People jump to help you in sympathy when you have problems. But nobody has any sympathy for me. Nobody has any sympathy for me!"

I had to run out of that house, or I would kill him. Going up and down the hills of those suburbs, I saw everything in red. My sides were hurting like a motherfucker. I got to Mrs. Eulalah's and told her my side, and that's when she called you to handle it, or she was going to handle it with her .45. The basement I was talking to you about before is where I'm writing you. It's the only place that makes sense in the world for me. What do I do, professor? What the fuck do I do with the rest of the world?

• • •

Dear Professor Thompson

I appreciate that you reached out

I've been okay the last few weeks. I'm just doing what Mrs. Eulalah tells me to do and living in her basement. She decked it out for a brother: I got a couch and a little TV, and I use Mrs. Eulalah's old kitchen and shower in the back room. It's too late to apply for a dorm in the fall quarter, but I'm looking to move to the Pierce dorms in winter. But I'm happy here, professor, and have everything I need.

I have a routine here, and I love it. In the morning, I help with the packages and make sure Miss Nona gets her iced mocha espresso and her sandwich from the breakfast truck. In the afternoons, I get my various orders from everybody and make sure Aisha gets her green smoothies from the food area in the Lowe's down the street. After work, I make sure everybody gets fish sandwiches and I grab a Coca-Cola Slurpee for Mrs. Eulalah to chase her Crown Royal. I speak when spoken to, but people appreciate me and are allowing me to speak more. To keep it real, I can breathe here. It feels healthy.

I gave a lot of thought to the offer to come back to the house. Believe me, sir; I respect that you want to counsel the family and help us get better. But I have to say no as graciously as possible. I can't put into words how much I admire the work you've done for me in helping me evolve from being a thug to a college student and decent citizen. If you want to meet with us outside of me going back into that house, I would make room in my schedule for the family to make that happen.

I've been talking to Aunt Estelle, and she tells me how sorry he is about what happened, so I will do my best to abide by her. I believe you when you said you had to give it great thought as to leaving him or not. I trust you when you tell me you offered the men's class to Dr. Everett not as a suggestion but as an ultimatum, given his history as a father figure to you. Because of all these things, I will continue to take his Black Humanities 101 class.

However, you are the one who told me to set up personal boundaries, and it was out of respect to my boundaries that I cannot go back to that house right now. Mrs. Eulalah and the sisters give me a sense of life outside of the streets and the political atmosphere of that house. It helps me heal myself when I can run errands for them. It isn't some hypothetical theory/rambling on the internet shit; it's something I can recognize. It's not like Mrs. Eulalah's is run by a bunch of right-wing motherfuckers; the shop talks about racism and the Man like it's the air. But the way people deal with it, the way people work around it and live their lives feels like real life to me. It would fuck me up sometimes to be in that house and talk about the struggle every single minute of every single motherfucking day. I didn't have any air, sir.

I'm also becoming more aware of things in regard to Dr. Everett. He's been talking about the Black Brilliance Project and their three-million-dollar panel. Well, so have the sisters at the shop. And they hate it. More than that, they hate the copycats on top of Everett. They say they have been paying attention to him and their bunch is —and I quote Nona—, "a group of niggas that have no proof of relationships with the cultural organizations in the communities they claim to represent, yet use the history of said groups to make demands. A group that has made a painfully open-ended financial demand for racial equity, yet continually fails to produce a sentence upon how that money will be spent, who gets it, or how this open-ended money will help said communities in the long run."

I don't want to believe them, I still appreciate what the family has done for me. I can't say this shit enough: you and Dr. Everett are braver than me (or at least, have been). I can't judge you too much because of the shit I did sticking up old ladies. You and him were doing adult shit getting up at four in the morning at the same age. I also understand that he's gone through a bunch of shit in school and has never got the proper respect for the critical theory work that he's done. But I still wince at how bad he beat me. And I can't get out of my head how bad he beat Aunt Estelle. I must respect her wishes even though I struggle with them. But I should have taken Mrs. Eulalah at her word when she said, "don't make him a Jesus."

I just want a lot more control over my own life and healing, professor. You were the one who said that I wouldn't be able to grow if I didn't fully process what happened to me and my life and my hand in it. I just can't do that in a place where I have to be that in that man's PR team. And I spent so much time in the house doing just that. I hope I still can be able to talk to you, professor. I have grown so much from our talks.

•••

Professor

I saw the *Black Psychiatry Journal* link that profiled you and wept like a baby when I was writing in Starbucks before work. I had never seen you open up about what you had to go through. I didn't know how your daddy got on that shit and died, how your mama struggled with health issues and what happened to her, and how you struggle to talk outside of your comfort zone. I hold my anger toward Dr. Everett because he was a father to you, and I see you are working out some shit right now. The shop was talking about it too and was getting emotional, though Mrs. Eulalah wished you would have more of a presence and stop making an obsession with searching for a father. She loves you too, dawg. She just wants you to be around more.

I want to be more like you than him right now. You are the one who put in the most work to help me past my criminal stage and become a college brother. I'm glad that Aunt Estelle said you can come with us shopping, and we can have weekly discussions that aren't family shit. Mrs. Eulalah and her sisters in the shop appreciate you when you are there so they can have one more brother to listen to them. I'm happy Aunt Estelle's even thinking of going to school again. It has been so wonderful to have her around and hear her and Mrs. Eulalah tell stories about the things she and my mom used to do. I'm glad they patched their shit out, even though they're a little more tense than they used to be. I used to think of Aunt Estelle as a proper, elegant person, and to hear her telling stories about shooting craps and fighting dudes surprised the shit out of me and made me laugh my ass off.

One last thing before our next meeting: the next time you see Dr. Everett, please tell him to stop focusing on those wack-ass videos and get his shit together about the class. Those videos are played, man. And I don't know what the syllabus is going to look like; I would just not like it to become reflective of his personal-ass shit with his ex-wife. I used to like it when he talked about how Aunt Estelle was his somebody to heal his pain and how important it was to find somebody who was your somebody, no matter the circumstances. I would like him to resume focusing on the present and the future instead of talking incessantly about how dysfunctional his relationship was with his "Jewish ex-wife." I still have a lot of hopes for the family.

I still hope we can re-bond and that we can do a lot of healing. Please believe me, even though I don't live in their house, I still want that. But I want a different goal of healing.

• • •

Professor

In class today, I thought of our ice cream therapy socials at Baskin-Robbins. I thought of you talking about being a moderating presence in Dr. Everett's class when you were his assistant. I did this because your presence was missed.

It started when he called me into his office before class. The first weird thing to me was that it was all decked with Africa, Marcus Garvey, Black Panther, and Black Power shit. I mean, I'm not saying there is anything wrong with that, but Everett's been more of an Obama, suit-and-tie nigga to me than this shit, and most of the stuff that it got was new shit that he got at the swap meet.

He passes me a coffee and starts talking, "you know Albert, you don't think I understand you, but I do. I lived in your neighborhood. I felt the anger you felt as a young Crip, and I still feel the anger at times. And for the longest time, I thought I had found a way to process it. For the longest time, I believed that I could process it by being three times as good as any White man to make it in America and academia. I thought it was my way to heal, and I thought it was the way for Black people to be successful. For the longest time, I was a good respectable boy with a good White liberal girl and believed that we were the best of our races and going to make a new world. But I got so burnt out, Albert."

He opened his window curtain and pointed to the big main office, "I've taken shit from them for 25 years. I spent 15 years, and I haven't made a quarter without a professor or a board member making a kitchen help joke. First administration meeting I had, the former dean asked me to get him coffee. First author's conference I had at the Seattle Marriott, I get to the door and a blue blood gives me her fucking keys in front of the whole auditorium. As if I'm the fucking valet. I try to be the liberal they want me to be for years. For years. and I lose count of the White academics who act surprised that I could read, or knew a White writer. I headline a symposium of Northwest memoirs, and the panel head says I'm there to steal wallets." Dr. Everett sat down in his old office chair and popped his feet on the corner of the desk. I didn't know what to say, so I took a sip of the coffee, but it was black and too strong for me, so I set it down.

"Yes, Albert, I took it and smiled for a while just yassud and nossud all them little blue bloods. Did everything I could to keep my goddamn nose clean. And for what, Albert? We have these goddamn glorified lynching bees with all our young boys getting shot on these goddamn streets, and here I have been some sad negro tying myself into the knots trying to get White folks to like me. I spent so much in my life being this happy negro teacher, happy that we could have a Black history curriculum, happy that some big wig administration would allow me to teach my students that a Black person had done something." He suddenly swung his feet off the desk with a bang and leaned forward to look at me. His intensity made me lean back a little.

"But I've changed, and I started changing a long time ago. That's why I left Miriam. She didn't love civil rights; she just loved Blacks who were punching bags. A goddamn sado-masochist weeping for the negro poor, but so squeamish when they want to rise up and fight their oppression. And I wanted to fight my oppression. I wanted to have agency! I wanted to do something for my people. That's why I started the studies department!" He got up and started pacing around the room. "That's why I led student protests to get more funding. That's why I built a better curriculum than any Black professor in the history of Nisqually. Who started teaching African and African American history books written by actual African and African Americans? Me!" he pumped his thumb into his chest so hard I heard it bounce. "Who built the syllabus people now use for the Underground Railroad, Reconstruction, the Harlem Renaissance, and the Civil Rights Movement. Me, that's who! And did Miriam or any tenured negro help me? Did any of these head-scratching 'I assure your Mr. Chancellor we're gradualists' negroes sit down with me man-to-man to help Black students?" He shook his head, but it looked like he was acting, like he was practicing a one-man play for me.

"I couldn't compromise, Albert. I couldn't compromise anymore. I was going crazy with the pain. And my woman didn't believe or understand me. She tried to tell me some bullshit about our shared values and Black people and Jews being blues people. But I was so tired.

Since I was a child I had been dealing with White folks, and I couldn't deal with them like this anymore. And like every fucking phony White liberal with a grudge, she's come back with a vendetta against me. After 25 fucking years, she gets to be the head of the humanities department and starts giving me this list of shit that I need to do. She starts telling me that I need to publish more. No one could write the novel I wrote, goddamn it. But she tells me that I need to put in more work. And that she comes off with this bullshit about how I need to include more Black women and liberal Whites." He finally stopped his pacing and stared off across the lawn to the fancy old admin building on the other side.

"But I'm going to show her, Albert. I'm going to give her the most militant fucking syllabus she's ever seen and dare her to fire me. I dare her to fucking fire me, in this environment we have? When it's open season and our young Black men? I dare her to fucking fire me right now. She's got the nerve to talk to me about identity politics, political correctness, the role of good liberals to fight this president, and embracing America as if the country ain't got no motherfucking problems. Well, I'm going to give her ass a motherfucking problem."

"And the thing is, the thing is, Albert, it fits right into the standards of critical inquiry. I'm a good, enlightened brother who has accomplished so much in his life. It takes a horrible set of traumas and circumstances to lay me low, to make me hit my Black queen. I know you kids love Baldwin so much, more than he loved being a token lapdog for New York neo-liberal; but he was right about one thing: Oppression doesn't breed saints, it breeds monsters. So I'm gonna talk about how it bred dysfunction for Black men, and what women like her..."

And after that, I just zoned out for a while. After a time, class is about to start and I go to my seat. Everybody comes in and he passes out the syllabus. And then goes into the same lecture he gave me with just a little more of Donald Trump in it. It still came off as a little unhinged to me, but I look around and it seems like everyone's just eating it up. And then I read the motherfucking syllabus. LeRoi Jones? Eldridge Cleaver? Frantz Fanon? Ed Bullins? Professor, I'm the last nigga on Earth to talk, given my criminal record of robbing old ladies when I was thirteen. However, I still remember some of my mother's literary sermons. I didn't go to college to read a bunch of niggas talking about taking and messing up pussy. And I'm supposed to "understand their pain" and "understand their revolutionary anger." I could get this shit from Big Thomas. I know we talked about his ex-wife problem in class, and he nodded and said he'd work on himself. I'm scared as hell that *this* is working on himself.

So I'm in a daze, trying to process this bullshit "take the pussy" class and process what the fuck last five years of rehabilitation have been, when I look up to see Judith looking at me. I somehow didn't notice her in the class of thirty. I had sat in the fifth row and was reading the syllabus when she walked past to leave. When I saw her look at me, I turned my head away in shame and sadness when she said, "why are you sad?"

" 'Cause this class is kinda bullshit."

"You mean to tell me you think it's not macho enough?"

"No," I sneered, "the opposite. I know I ain't shit. You know I ain't shit. But one thing I do know is a nigga who ain't shit. And these niggas right here?" I shook the syllabus at her, "these niggas right here ain't shit."

"So you're here looking sad for the same reason that I am?"

"I think so."

"Going to be a long quarter."

"Yeah."

She comes up the steps to my row and sits right next to me. I attempt to say I'm sorry again, and she puts an index finger in front of her lips. We sat in silence long after the students were gone, looking at the chalkboard.

"Look, I know I ain't shit a lot of ways, but..."

"Who gave you that scar Albert?" she pointed to my left eye, reminding me of when the professor opened it in our fight. As I struggled to find out what to say, she looked down at the syllabus, gave a deep sigh, then stretched her hand out to me.

"I'm trying to understand," I said.

"So am I."

I still am, professor. You got to help me make sense of this. Make this make sense for me. I believed you when you said you begged him to change the syllabus. I want to help, be a plus in the situation, and be part of a solution for this family. But I want to be part of things that make sense. Please help me make sense of this.

• • •

Professor

The shop misses you, and they would love to see you stop by in a capacity that isn't fixing a problem or taking me in and out of men's group. Nona speaks of what you used to do here fondly, and Aisha says that she still appreciates the books you used to recommend to her. I see the proof in the pudding that you talked about in regard to character when they speak about you. I'm sorry, but I don't see it in Dr. Everett anymore. I get what you said when you told me, "you got to let people process their traumas." But the more he does it, the less it feels like him explaining his life and more like him waving a golden ticket and shit. Or worse, when he starts to cry and starts to talk about how he is a child of society. Or how he's such a male feminist for recognizing it and wanting a cookie for being imperfect. Or worse than that, when he decides to go on his YouTube channel and air out all of our private business for the social media world to see.

To keep it 100, I'm beginning to entertain ideas of easing out of the class. It's just too stressful to have day-to-day interactions with the family. The Black humanities class is such a pain in the ass and double so because ass-kicking James and Darren came into it late, and that shit takes up so much of my energy. I will say that I appreciate you teaching me not to look at women as friends and not sex packets. I really appreciate getting to know Judith as a person because she's the only person that understands how fucked up the class is. When she told me her life story about her daddy being a soldier in Auburn and struggling with PTSD, and raising her and her brothers by herself, I sobbed more than any time, except for the time when I found out my mama died.

She took me to the VFW soup kitchen as my own atonement friendship ceremony. Going there yesterday was more of a humanities education than anything I've learned from Everett. For one thing I wasn't predisposed to feel like a king or a prodigal, but a servant. I know I suffered, and I know our people suffered, but I get tired of hearing only how we suffer. I'm getting tired of a lot, professor.

•••

Professor

I'm sorry I didn't go to the "Black Fire" protest art opening like you wanted me to, but I had to draw a line. I know you want me to try to ingratiate myself with the students more, but I just don't want to give my time to the piece. I mean, a furnace, metal planks painted black that look like ramps with rocks black and white all over them? I get the symbols and shit, they think we are in a dreary-ass race war funded by capitalism, and I'm not saying it doesn't have merit. But Macalester had invited me and the shop to her TV night, and it was my responsibility to make chicken wings. I'm really doing good with the shop and getting closer to people. Eulalah is letting me run errands with her, and I appreciate the responsibility.

I have to deal with my chores or classes, the errands that I need to do for the shop every day, plus write the correct radical answers for Dr. Everett's "I hate my White ex-wife" class. I've even talked about it with Mrs. Eulalah, and she says that I have to leave but gracefully, that I have to back away without making an announcement. I want to be respectful of what they've done for me for the last five years because they did get me out of Juvie. And I don't forget that. Honest to God, though, I wish that our sessions didn't feel like internet branding for him.

• • •

I hope the next time we have a conversation I can respectfully give the other side of the story of what happened with Aunt Estelle and Kyle at Mrs. Eulalah's. You know how much I love Aunt Estelle. And I'm working through my feelings with Kyle. I want to see him win, stop acting like a wanna-be Crip, and take advantage of the good things in his life, and I'm glad he's trying to do that. But as somebody who was there, what they said happened didn't happen. I was scared to say anything because they were both so angry and hurt and heartbroken, and you had told me to work on not interrupting women.

With all that said, professor, what they said happened didn't happen. They didn't come into the shop only to be instantly thrown out. He did come in with the money he raised from working at the pizza shop to pay for the TV he broke, but he did it in the middle of the day when the shop was running behind, one of the chairs wasn't working, the truck that came in to bring us activator didn't come, people were just in a generally bad mood, and Aunt Estelle and Kyle came in just demanding everyone's attention. It had only been a few months, and they came in expecting that she and the shop were going to forgive so damn easily.

And yes, she did not. "You better take that burnt cork, punk-ass, vanilla ice ass nigger out of my goddamn shop." Eulalah came like she was going to push the two right out the door.

"I just wanted him to come in to give restitution for your TV," said Aunt Estelle, "and what the hell? Who the hell are you talking to?"

"He can do that another motherfucking time and a motherfucking time comfortable. I'm tired of your bougie ass coming in here expecting people to drop everything for you. And I know exactly who the hell I'm talking to. Call me for an appointment that's comfortable for me. I can't deal with you or your golf course gangbanger son today."

"Jesus Christ, Eulalah. This is me. You know me. You know my son. All the times I brought him here as a little boy."

"But he ain't a little boy no more. And yo ass what is bothering me in the shop right now."

"Bothering you? You have no right to say that I'm bothering you."

"I don't have a right? Why?"

"It's because... It's because... because you know me..."

"All I did to provide you with a place to go to school, and I have no right. All the books about you and I have no right. All the times I fed you, took you to the scholarship dinner, made sure you had the right clothes and the right everything for you to raise up from Hillside Terrace, and I have no right."

"That's not where I'm going. I'm just saying that you know my son."

"Just because you married some high-grade Hotep conscious Nigger, you think you better than me. Vonetta, God rest her soul, was batshit crazy but would talk to me. We would have conversations. We used to have conversations longer than you and I had conversations. But ever since you went to the suburbs, you look at me like the help."

"Don't you fucking dare say that after all the years you've had with me."

"What you going to do? You got to come in here when I'm stressed out of my mind, we three motherfuckers behind schedule, the activator hasn't come in yet, and I'm supposed to stop and jump for joy because your sad sack of a son in the suburbs knows how to act for two months and went eight weeks without calling somebody a bitch?"

"Where is this all coming from? Have you lost your mind?"

"Oh, I'm a crazy bitch now. Get the hell out of my shop."

"We just walked in the door and had eye contact, and you bit my head off within seconds. I can't tell you how my family is getting better? I can't tell you that my family is getting better for a few seconds?" Aunt Estelle was clutching the envelope full of money in front of her.

"Oh, oh, I'm a monster; yes, yes, I'm the monster. Just go. I have given you all I can. I have given you so much. I can't give any more. I just can't give to your ass anymore." And with that she turned her back on Aunt

Estelle and went back to work like she wasn't even there. Aunt Estelle lingered a moment, then her face just broke and she walked out with Kyle tagging after.

We worked the rest of the day, and Mrs. Eulalah didn't say a word to no one. Macalester came in from a pride rally and got some activator from Puyallup, and things slowly got together. The shop was quieter, and everything was starting to run smoothly. Everybody left, and I was about to go right when she broke down.

"I'm so tired, Albert. I'm so tired. She brought that kid around the shop, but she didn't invite me to the hospital when that boy was born. She didn't invite me to the baby shower. She can't stop talking about 'how come the women in the shop don't love her anymore.' That we don't love her like we used to. That we drift away because of the suburbs. Albert, we didn't drift away 'cause she went to the suburbs. We drifted away because she thought she was better than us when she married that professor. She got her English degree and just became a University Place housewife, expecting to get compliments every time she came into this room. And I mean every time. She acted like her life was over, and she was some sort of a queen. I know she had to climb some places to get where she had to get to. But didn't I help her? Did I not give anything to her? I gave and gave and gave, and it's never enough for her ass. I'm so tired, Albert. I'm just so tired."

• • •

Professor

I'm starting to get emotional and almost reverential around Aisha, not because I want to go with her, but because she reminds me of my mama. Last week, when she went off on a tangent about Claude Brown, I heard my mother talking and had to check and compose myself.

Yesterday was a trip and half too, boss. It was an hour after close, and I was trying to write another morally compromised essay for the class, when an answer to a prompt you gave that I struggled with hit me. It was about seven, I was trying to find the fourth way of saying, "even though I find these actions reprehensible, I understand and respect this Black man's pain." Macalester was outside in full camouflage armor playing solitaire in her Gran, and Aisha was working on marketing shit on her laptop. The music had just stopped, and instead of putting on something else, Aisha closed her laptop and looked at me. "Albert, have you ever looked outside in this hour?"

"Not really, though I know we close on Friday because of the high school bros."

"That's not what I mean. You've been in the suburbs a few years and did time in the lower rungs in the Trap. Take a look at the parking lot and tell me what you see. You want to be a writer like your momma, right? Then you need to learn to observe. Take some time to observe."

I went to the window and watched how the line became a system. I saw how Black drug dealers from the hill would dress in their finest gear to jockey a position to sell their product to an expensive clientele. The usual dope fiends would go to Value Village and buy their best clothes to bullshit their way in, but the upper crust didn't fall for their schtick.

"Every Friday, I see people from the neighborhood's fortunes falling week by week, payday by payday, with the police around here not doing shit." Aisha put her arm across the window and rested her forehead on it, "just this year I saw a big, strong Safeway butcher turned into shriveled up skin and bones before my eyes. A doe-eyed married couple of white-collar professionals grew to be bug-eyed and divorced. Aspiring students turned into denizens, deacons turned the deviants, cheerleaders turned into crackheads, and football stars turned into freebase junkies as the market here serves as death's slow, painfully slow extension. And I've seen this shit since I was a little girl.

"And it made me so angry," she got two sodas from the cooler Mrs. Eulalah had in the first chair. "I had it good growing up in the apartment complex up on the outskirts up the road, but all these motherfuckers made me want to go to Hillside Terrace. The minute they knew about my momma and her almost rap group, they came to me as if they was Robbie fucking Crusoe, and I was their bitch Friday. I was their bitch that could help them get goodies in their rap adventures, and every time they asked me, I wanted to kill them. If It wasn't for Mrs. Noland at Nisqually Prep that convinced me to quit hating White people, I might be one of the students you hate. Made a whole syllabus for my ass of White writers who were poor. Sinclair to Steinbeck to Allison. She told me not to hate pigment but hate systems. She got into my face and challenged me when I took her humanities class and taught me to centralize my anger so it wouldn't have power over me.

"That's why I get heated when I talk in the book club," she stepped out to give Macalester a soda through the open car window, then leaned against the brick wall of the shop, I follow. "I'm processing a lot so I don't have to be that protestor. I'm processing in front of you because I trust you. Why doesn't Andre understand that?"

"Why you say that?" I asked.

"He spends more time trying to save that professor than talking and relating to us," she said to her and me. "He gets along here well, but he would get along better if he just—"

"Don't tell your mama's business," Macalester said from the car.

• • •

It was good for the shop that you got Mrs. Eulalah and Aunt Estelle back together. You should run for office or try to be a diplomat for that shit. Swear to God, you were talking to them and engineering everything as if you were on C-SPAN. I don't know if it's gonna stick, but the end result is the shop loves you more than they did yesterday (and that they loved you a lot yesterday). Those two have too much history to be completely cut off. They talk a lot of shit to each other, but I can tell you, from knowing them both, that they are miserable when they have distance. Also, thank you for allowing me to quit the group by telling Dr. Everett that I had sufficient growth. You really did me a solid on that one.

Life at the shop is pretty fucking wonderful, but sometimes the blues gets me. It happened one night after work when Nona told me a little bit about the group she used to be in, but not in a direct way.

"Take out the electric piano from the woodshed," she told me.

"We ain't got no electric piano."

"We do as of yesterday." She threw me two dollars, "bring it in, then get us coffee cream smoothies from the stand out front."

I hauled it in, got the order, then opened the door to see her playing gospel chords. I sat on the couch across from her and watched her awhile, till she stopped and looked at me. "You still doing Andre's lessons?"

"Yes ma'am" I said.

"You know your mama, Estelle, and I came from the same church."

"No I did not."

"Reverend Minister Zeke Clayton. My granddaddy. A Vesuvius of rage. Got a degree in business, spent a decade in the armed forces, and served his country in Korea. Did all this between 1944 to 1953 with all the physical and emotional scars to prove it. And when he came back to civilian life after he served his country, after he had decorations and laurels in the top percentile of any men, the best job he could get was co-running a cola plant with a White man. And he couldn't deal with it. Punched a White man out, did time, and only felt he had two choices with his binary mind of his: out-Nation the Nation of Islam or run to a right-wing Jesus. A hard nigga, Albert. My grandaddy was a hard nigga." She kept riffing on the piano, fusing jazz, stride, and gospel, leaning toward parts of certain songs, yet changing before she could play a whole one. It was captivating as hell, the first time I really could see how she used to be a performer. I was on the edge of the couch listening.

"That's what my big mama saw. That's what my daddy and mama saw before they saw some needles. I'm sure big mama is still trying at that church. She came up from Detroit, the daughter of a two-bit player and a little girl too young to have her. And she bounced around orphanages till she saw the army recruit as a chance for stability. And when she got here, she saw my father as a chance for stability. My father was educated, clean-cut, and handsome, offered her a chance for a better life, and told her she was more moral than any White woman." her playing changed to a minor key, "but when she married him and submitted to his God, all she got was work orders. 'Why isn't this house spotless? Why is my steak overcooked? Why are you bigger than the church wives I see in University Place?' And all I got was work orders. 'Why aren't your shoes spotless? Why isn't your dress pressed right? Why is your diction not proper in your songs?' And if I was anything less than perfect, if my mother was anything less than perfect, the nigga would haul off, then tell us he was doing it because we were blocking our people's pilgrimage to the promised land. That we were negating our responsibilities to break the color bar in the Fircrest suburbs and hurting every Black boy and girl and every Black person in Tacoma." Nona stopped her noodling on the keyboard and looked at me.

"And I believed, Albert. For the longest time, I wanted to believe. 'Cause to believe something else was to process my momma and daddy being gone, and I couldn't do that. With my momma being a better spokesperson for Him than Him, I jumped through all the hoops because I was a child, I was in a special position and this was what I was supposed to do. We would do our dishes and chores, and she would paraphrase over his rough rants in a way that made his demands bearable. When we were done, we would sit at the table, and she would say that I was a good little girl, how much all our work was going to pay off, and how we were on our way to be in heaven." She started the music up again. It had a slower tempo now; still gospel but more of a funeral hymn.

"I was overwhelmed with the fear of race failure, Albert. I was supposed to be in a tap recital that I had practiced for two months, and I felt enough pressure to lose my third-grade mind. I was supposed to do the tap dance number in to 'I'm Happy's Because It's In My Nature,' " she plonked out a few bars of the song, it was so upbeat it put your hair on end, mimicking the hook until she slammed her hands on the keys. "Fuck. And I was supposed to do it because University Place White folks were mad at the King Holiday, and if I showed I was a docile negro who sang a docile negro song, people would look at the Reverend as a negro leader again. Yes, if I did this on point; did the perfect number, on the perfect cues, smiling the perfect amount of times, the White people would see our humanity and let more negroes in the school. To strive toward that goal, Albert, he made me practice till my twelve-year-old feet bled.

"That whole day of the recital, I can't hold a goddamn thing in. I throw up, then feel bad that I am going to let down my people, then throw up some more on account of me feeling bad. I hallucinate in class, the halls, and the bathroom, I see people laughing at me real and imagined, and I hear my grandaddy's disappointing voice like an echo. And then I see Eulalah, who went to the wrong end of the building and the hill to register for the ROTC meeting." The music changed up-tempo, wandering to something between gospel and soul, like the James Cleveland songs my mother used to curse at on the radio, going faster and faster till she took a deep breath, stopped playing and looked at the first chair.

"Before that day, I had heard my grandfather preach about the peril of female power in a godless society, of Lot and Babylon, and those lost women he saw on the outskirts of Moncks Corner juke joints, ripe to be picked up by White boys cruising. And there, there in these secular school hallways was a woman who had a general's uniform, or what looked like a general's uniform to me. In my nerves and fever, I thought I'd died a sinner. Yet she kept waving me toward her, with these eyes of concern.

" 'You okay, baby?' she asked, kneeling in front of me.

" 'I... I have to...'

" 'You don't have to do nothing, sugar,' but I kept nodding as she grabbed my head, 'Jesus Christ. What did they do to your hair?'

" 'I have to be the best little girl and sing my best little song.'

" 'Conk! Lye! Did niggas put lye in your head, sugar?' and she gave me this huge hug.

" 'Yes, ma'am,' I said.

" 'I got a beauty shop, baby. You want me to try and fix this?'

"And something in me said yes before I could remember my church training. I remember her taking me to her office and agreeing that she was my aunt. I remember how she guided my tired self to the front seat of her car, then her buckling me in, then going past all the hills of University Place I had seen only in buses, then stopping at her shop. I remember her clearing a path to the wash sink and giving her orders for the chairs and customers. 'Estelle, heat the iron to half. Sarah, get mama's masks from the basement. The one that say 'First Baptist Women's Day, Galveston.' Vonetta, stop stewing and get the bond formula. Ann, get the placement gel from my table. Helen, take this $40 and get us the bird and rib special at Bob's. You hungry baby?'

"And I started to say, 'no, I have to do my recital and be a good Christian girl and with a good weight,' but I felt myself in the water. And saw these faces that had so much care in them. These wayward, secular faces wearing different forms of clothes and hair who didn't want nothing from me. And I felt Eulalah rub my head over and over." She turned the power switch off like an act of reverence and the gentle hum died out.

"That's where I began my life, Albert. That's where I learned care. This is why I want to someday help people get a place, not necessarily my place, but a place where their lives will start."

"Counseling?" I asked.

"Yeah, but Eulalah says I can do that in first chair. I don't know how to bridge that. I don't know how to bridge it with Andre either, who makes overtures about us doing it together, but I can't abide by the self-taught Black macho... I mean I love him, but... Let's change the subject."

She stopped and looked outside for a minute. The night coffee stand must of heard her playing and turned their music off, but now they put on some Anita Baker. I smiled.

"Albert, I don't know another brother your age who likes *The Quiet Storm* that much."

"Yes, ma'am."

"Trying to impress a young girl? Only brothers I see looking like Joe College listening to *The Quiet Storm* working hard to impress a young woman."

"Nah, It's not like that. I'm not trying to flirt with Aisha."

"Boy, I didn't say you were. I just want to know why you like the music you like."

"I... I like it because it's calming. I got a lot of shit on my mind. I don't blame my fuckup actions on it, but I got a lot of shit on my mind. I used to be a fuck up, and I'm working on not doing all the things I used to do."

"I get it. Let's go get a fish sandwich."

As we walked toward the fish truck, she looked at my book for Dr. Everett's class (which I hate more every waking day). It was Richard Wright's *Eight Men*, a book of stories that reflected more on his anger toward his separated, White ex-wife (shocker!). "We had that at book club one time," Nona said. "What do you think of it?"

"To keep it a buck, I'm tired of reading niggas so weak in the face of racism, they end up wanting to kill all the White ladies."

"And their Black partners. That's a big thing with Aisha. In school, when she got to the part in *Native Son* where Bigger also kills his Black girlfriend, cuts her up, and puts her in the furnace, she yelled to the teacher, 'AND WHATS THE *POLITICAL REASON* FOR THIS?!' What I'm getting to, in relation to the first question that I asked, is that Black women have to deal with great men's ghosts. I was in a rap group that was almost famous, and I got a lot of shit from it. The reason Eulalah doesn't have hip-hop anything in the shop is that men used to recognize me from the group, come in and badger me about their mixtapes, and get hostile when Eulalah and I said no. They couldn't take no, Albert. They wanted to touch and be affirmed by greatness (or what they thought was greatness) and got so damned hostile when they heard the reality and my reality. But reality is something I had to deal with, Albert. The archetype of the great men that you will hear Aisha roaring about at times is something she and we have to deal with every day. We have to deal with the actual of these niggas and the dichotomy between the actual in what men believe is the actual of these niggas."

I nodded and, as we turned back, I saw a little boy being coached by his mother before he went into the corner store. She held him by the shoulders like Mrs. Eulalah holds me when I need instruction or correction. But I looked at his backpack and school uniform, and I started to break. I saw myself, professor. I saw myself if I had courage. I saw myself If I took those ass whuppings you took and helped my mother get healthy. I saw me in college and my mother teaching and us reading by the hidden lake.

I saw in all clarity an alternative universe, and when it was gone, I wanted to go back. I closed my eyes, and I started to pray. I started to pray and speak in tongues I didn't know I had. I willed my mind to dig past the present, my own cowardice, and my tenuous-ass future to give me the redo God hadn't granted anyone else in the world. On my knees, I begged in tongues with all the force of my soul. Hot flashes emanated from my body that felt like the fires of hell, and I closed my eyes and saw the court sequence again and the nightmarish finality of the last time I saw her. After that I remember Nona sitting next to me in the parking lot with the food truck lady, "oh, Albert," she said, touching my face, "forgiving yourself is a hard hustle."

• • •

Professor Thompson,

Yeah. I quit Everett's fucking class. And this was before the interracial shaming list those students shared with Reed College online. It's one thing to listen to these motherfuckers whine about White people every day. Now I got to get on a collective Prep School shit list because I don't want to slap Judith with my dick. I've been around the book club and the "discourse" at the beauty shop far too goddamn long to pretend that this "let's feel sorry for activists who want to take pussy" class isn't a waste of my motherfucking time.

I can't say this enough, professor. I'm the last nigga on earth to say they don't have a right to be angry. I have a bunch of motherfucking stories about the man and the Tacoma PD feeling my nuts when I was nine years old. And if one gave a good goddamn look at the thirty open minutes of the day when they just rant because Dr. Everett wants to find points to riff off racism and his Jewish ex-wife, there are ten where they have some credible points. I'm not immune to the shit of the world for us. I've lost count who every Black person who's been shot by police and neighborhood watch for some bullshit. And I have lost count of the number of White people I've seen who put them on trial for their own murder.

But those other twenty minutes are kicking my ass, professor. If the shop and hanging out with Judith taught me anything, it's that you got to have antennas to take in the good shit in life. Sometimes it's an impromptu after-work dance party. And sometimes it's a Joni Mitchell song that you listen to for the first time and want to know everything about. And sometimes it's a poem by Emily Dickinson that got a lot of dope images that you can just lose yourself in. And if you say that in class, almost all of the time, twenty out of thirty people gonna call you an unwoke Uncle Tom. And eight are scared to say anything. And the remaining two people are Judith and me.

It doesn't stop there, professor! Have you heard of #cancelmayaangelou? 'Cause I have. Or how about #cancelgladysknight? Or #cancelchakakhan? Or even #cancelsteviewonder? And do you know every White poet who has made a mistake on race? (Or what negroes and holier-than-thou White folks who can afford Nisqually think is a mistake on race?) 'Cause I do, and it's all because of this class. For all this shit he talked about trying to change the syllabus and focus on his anger in our sessions, all he did was dump the stress, tensions, and obsessions that made me hate that house on all the students and made them want to talk to people about their lord and savior, #blacktwitter.

And of course, the college Republicans ain't shit. Judith and I went to a meeting, and it was just a bunch of punk-ass proud boys and blue-blood neurotics who can't speak five sentences without trying to "own a lib." But I just wish that our class would do something constructive. I just wish I could see more of my fellow students trying to reach people instead of the shame cycle group sessions. And I just wish they would just get the fuck off of Judith's ass. I know she ain't a motherfucking wallflower: She's told me as such. But if we had a class curriculum with a bunch of White people saying it was okay to Big Thomas me and cut off my junk, I'd be on edge too.

I know what you're probably saying, "get to the part where you lost your shit." We were going over the part in *Soul on Ice* where Eldridge writes the fake-ass love letter to Black women (after he talked about raping women for practice earlier). Well, week seven of the same back and forth happened: Judy and I said Eldridge was on some inexcusable bullshit like we said with Richard Wright and LeRoi Jones/Baraka/Waka Flakka-whatever the fuck he called himself. The rest of the class went off on how Judith doesn't understand how racism can anger and overwhelm a man and how I'm only saying what I'm saying because I wanted to fuck Judith. I saw her put her head down and just lost my shit.

And yes, that gets me a little bent because I remember what you taught me about friendship. And Judith needed a friend. Not a lover, but a goddamn friend. We usually spend an hour hanging out, but yesterday at the VF, she needed somebody to spend a day listening to her process shit. That's where she told me about her problems with her two younger brothers turning into red-pilled hellcats. There was a thicket of shit she had to process being basically the mom until she was sixteen and had to be taken in by a teacher in Nisqually Prep. And well, there ain't no damn demons in her family, but them two brothers she got ain't shit for calling her a beta cunt. So when the class went off the next day, I went a bit nuts because I was protective of her.

"I want each and every one of you Twitter niggas to hear me when I say this," I said, standing up and walking down the steps to the front of the class. "Ain't. Nothing. Going. On. Ain't. Nothing. Gonna. Go on. If one of you motherfuckers drop your embargo on reading White writers and read a psychology book —or, pray tell, take your asses to therapy— you might find the term 'relationship dynamic.' And in me and Judy's relationship dynamic is me being an abusive, misogynist, antisemitic bullying piece of shit to her in high school. That she has decided to be cordial and friendly to me reflects more on her character than it does on mine. And the key to our relationship dynamic being healthy is none of the fucking y'all think is happening... happening."

"Nigga, get off your high horse," said Darren, "you sitting here talking about some feminist shit, and you robbed a bunch of old ladies as a boy."

"You are the prototypical phony neo-liberal male feminist," said Sondra, James' girlfriend.

"Central casting, nigga," said James, "central casting."

"Oh, you right, Sondra," I said. "I ain't shit. I will try to live down my bullshit until the day I fucking die. My point is that y'all niggas ain't shit either. You got a right not to like my Black ass for what I did. And all the people in your family you complain about who don't like you because you say you're too woke got a right not to like your Black ass either. Cancel Maya Angelou? You want to cancel Maya Angelou five years after her body is in the ground. You want to cancel Maya Angelou because you saw a YouTube clip where she asked a student to call her 'Mrs. Angelou.' You call that 'being mean to a student.' Every nigga I know would call that 'you not having home training.' "

"Fuck you nigga. I'm not a dog."

"And if you knew as much about Black people as you said you do, you'd know I didn't call you one. James! Mr. #cancelgladysnight!"

"She went off on Colin Kaepernick!"

"Who went off for Huey Newton. Who got a Rolodex of murder and rape beefs."

"You fucking tool of the establishment," said Dr. Everett, interrupting James.

"I am? Is that right?"

"You don't understand what the government did to Black men who went against the system. You are a crazy-ass gangster in love with a White woman who doesn't understand a thing about COINTELPRO or anything I told you about the Black Panthers."

"Oh, I understand what you said, sir. I understood what you said so much I did more reading than what you told me to, and if you had any fucking guts, you'd tell them that the same COINTELPRO that jailed him was funding his apartment until he became a basehead who couldn't keep up his con."

"Bullshit."

"*Shadow Of The Panther.* Hugh Pearson. Published 1994."

"Bullshit."

"*The Party's Over.* Kate Coleman. New Times, 1978."

"Stop interrupting the class," said James.

"*Will You Die With Me?* Flores Forbes, 2006. Eldridge's later confessions. Pick a year after 1975. Write them down if you honestly give a fuck about the truth about Black life in this class."

"I don't care about Black life?" he scoffed. "Nigga get the hell out of mine. Get the hell out of mine and get the hell out of my life forever." And I skipped out that motherfucker like 2Pac skipped out of court.

I walked straight down to my hiding place in school. A small little table on the beach past the train tracks and the man-made lake. It's more dirty and dingy than most of the park tables in class, but it's a place where I can be alone and tranquil. Most of the time, I eat lunch and talk to my mother. I talked to my mother because that's where she drowned. I had sat down preparing to meditate and later compose what I was going to say to Mrs. Eulalah when I heard a voice. "You know how to make an exit, friend," said Judith.

"Now I got to figure out what to do."

"How about not being a stranger."

"That's doable."

"And work on your word choice. You complain that this is a 'take the pussy' syllabus. Which is correct, but the phrase 'Take the pussy' is coarse. It focuses too much on the taker. When you talk about Jones, Wright, and Cleaver, say the word rape. They raped people or talked about raping people."

"Gotcha."

"And whatever Big Thomas did to you, man. If you need permission from a woman to say it, you can. You can define whatever the fuck happened to you, but if you need permission to say it, you got it. That happened to you."

And I held her hand and said thank you. And then I heard Darren's "BAM! Gotcha bitch. All my shit is going on the internet."

Three days later, we were on the Reed, Nisqually, UW interracial sex shame list. 5,232 people poked and agreed on the statement I was a problematic man who had sex with White women and benefitted from the privilege.

Plus the nigga altered a video of me losing my shit in that class around comment 220, just playing a motherfucking tape of me yelling with the sound down so that nobody could decipher what I was saying (which made it look like it was just me marching to the front of the class and disrupting shit). Which is enough for me, dawg. É-nough. Y'all can work that out in your sessions with Daddy Everett, professor. Cause I ain't never coming back to them. Ever. Ever ever? Ever ever.

•••

Professor Thompson

Yo, I was about to write you this whole-ass email about how much I miss talking to you, how much the shop misses talking to you, and how the shop is worrying about you. Then I saw Kyle circling the block with some niggas his golf school gangsta ass shouldn't be circling with. Right outside Mrs. Eulalah's, I swear to God. Fucked up our entire day.

I still feel some shit about him, even though I feel bad when I do. He was just a kid who liked to wear black and play racing games on his Xbox when I met him; and even though he's a toxic little nigga, I still feel responsible for the cause and effect. I was the one in Dr. Everett's videos who was getting attention for being a reformed/not reformed thug, and when he doesn't show up by the shop, I feel sad for him. But then, just as I mention it, he shows up.

Before, we had had a good day and a fish fry after work, and we had spent the time working on me to get housing in two months before I had to go to bed, and I looked up to see Kyle in an old ass Sonics jersey surrounded by some real trap niggas in Jeeps.

You were on everybody's mind, especially Aisha's. She said, "what I can't understand, Albert, is how much he wants to save Scott to the detriment of himself."

"That's his daddy, baby," said Mrs. Eulalah. "That's the only nigga that stepped up or wanted to."

"She ain't lying," said Nona. "I was here when he worked here, and a lot of Black men in the vicinity called him a bitch for being sensitive and deferential to us. And Scott was the first elder man not to call him a bitch."

"Oh, he later called Estelle a bitch a few times. And I'm sure he calls you a bitch every other day. But yeah, he didn't call him a bitch."

"That's my point, though," said Aisha. "Macalester, you told me you'd learned how to fight to protect your mother from men who go prowling and harassing at the food bank."

"Yeah," she said.

"This ain't something foreign to you either, Albert," she said to me. "I mean before you got caught up."

"Yeah."

"One of the things you have to understand, Albert, is just because you are feeding starving people doesn't make you an untouchable chef. From what y'all have described to me, Scott —and I call the nigga Scott because he isn't my professor and isn't going to be—came in here and got enough of your lives to develop rhetoric to skate. He does the 'Black Queen Yada Yada Yada' article, the 'Black Women are Goddesses Yada Yada Yada' article, the 'Why I Love Black Women/Give Me All the Compliments Now Yada Yada Yada' article, and can't nobody tell him shit about his actions for the rest of his life. And there's a lot of niggas out there who do that, Albert. Niggas around the Red Square, the classroom, the club, in the church, willing to corner you with their talking points, expecting you to give a little something of your soul every time. And those niggas are corrosive. And I'm so scared, so scared that by not cutting off Scott, Andre will be corrosive someday as well."

"How did he leave?"

"You get too much in a bitch business," said Mrs. Eulalah. "I tell you the rules to this job, and you–"

"It's fine, Eulalah," said Nona. "I started to feel things when I didn't have an ounce of energy to feel things. He was handsome. Respectful. And protected us. But he was so young, Albert. And I had lost everything in my life and mind when the rap group went to hell and Aisha's father died. And I knew —I knew— that Andre, after his momma died, wasn't wrapped too tight. We were outside in the food trucks, and I was looking at all that light hazel in his eyes and in his cheekbones and sentences stopped forming well, and I didn't have the words to say 'I'm falling for you, but I'm exhausted out of my mind with my life right now.' And I just said he was too sensitive for me. That he was going through too much and I just wanted to support him as a friend. And he just nodded like a puppy, and left for Everett's during the summer."

"Is that why he incorporated Dr. Umar in his classes?" Aisha asked.

"He says he put it in a both sides/critical inquiry/class debate type of way."

Breaking the tension, some familiar-ass trap music, with some familiar-ass booming systems, rattled the windows. I look outside, and I see some familiar-ass niggas and the golf course gangsta himself. Let me put you up on game, professor: I was a runner who happened to run into a minor league buster perv. That minor league buster perv answered to ballers above his league. Kyle was surrounded by a bunch of ballers above my league and way above his, who want to use him and discard him when he is dispensable. I'm sorry to racially profile, maybe those niggas were stockbrokers, but if there is a nigga you know who knows niggas that are trapping, it's me. I have seen. This shit. Before. I don't know what ashy nigga Everett is worshipping in his class or what chapter of his pain he is talking about in yours, but please tell him that his little boy is in fucking trouble.

He gazes at me, looking outside the window, and I go outside to protect the shop. He comes out front, and the closer he gets to me, the more his knees buckle. "The fuck you doing, man?" I ask him.

"Could you get me out of this?"

"Get you out of this? Nigga I don't know those niggas, but I know those niggas are niggas I don't want to know. Those niggas will destroy your life, Kyle."

"Please help me."

"I can't help your ass," I walked back a few steps.

"Please, just act like I robbed you, or they will shoot me."

And after that, I gave him a $20. "You don't know me anymore, nigga. And none of those niggas should know me. You are a stupid nigga in a game you don't understand, and I can't get you out of it." Then he nodded, smirked, and ran off; and I turned back to see the shop looking right at me.

I swear to God, professor, I'm done with those niggas. I'll talk to Aunt Estelle every once in a while, but I'm done with everything else about the fucking family. I got to move on with my life and find new people. After this class, I'm just finished with this political hyper-woke shit. I swear to God I want you and Aunt Estelle in my life, and I appreciate the part you played in me growing. But a nigga got to find some new parts. I can't deal with this high-class family agony anymore, and I wonder why you can deal with it. You are the one who told me never to act like a society's child, yet your father is the most society's child nigga I've seen in my goddamn life. I don't mean to be mean, professor. I'm just processing. And I am just done with this. I am so done with everything that was my life for the longest time.

• • •

Dear Professor Thompson

Please believe me when I say I had nothing to do with getting Kyle in the trap game. I haven't done anything near that since my momma died, and I can't get her being gone out of my head. Being kicked out of the school and the shop has just broken me. I understand why people did what they did and why people have a hard time believing me. So I'll go away back on the streets. But it's killing me. Jesus Christ, it's killing me to think about it.

I know I don't have the most believable track record when I say he set me the fuck up. But he did. I didn't force him into the game. I repeat: he was the one who begged me to fake him robbing me and when he got caught with a bag cooked up a story saying that I gave him money to do it. Do you even believe that? Do you? Do you believe Kyle's crying act in the shop when he said that I was trying to start a "Power" like trap game in high school and college?

But anyway, I have to take it because he has "evidence" and Darren and James cosigning him because they want to be close to their Nationalist daddy. I don't know how those old rocks got back in my sweats, but he is her son and he and them two niggas say I put them there, and he says some shit like "my fingerprints are on his money." And I have to take it. I went to do yard work to help Aunt Estelle and left my dirty sweatpants, and I have to take it. It's fucking killing me, but I have to take it.

I've been hearing voices again ever since Estelle went to Eulalah's, and she kicked me out of her shop. I went to register for winter, and I found out that I wasn't enrolled anymore. Then I went to the dean's office to find out I was "suspended pending on an expulsion hearing", then took the bus to Mrs. Eulalah's to find out that I don't have a life anymore. And the only place that gave me a stable home don't want me no more. And the women I love more than anything are telling me that I'm a snake, a phony male feminist, and a typical woke abuser who used us. And that they will never trust another Black man because of me. And what can I tell them because of Darren and James? It fucking killed me more that I was such a fuck up that I can't say she hasn't got a right not to trust me. Hell, if I were her, I probably wouldn't. But I didn't. I swear to God I didn't get Kyle involved in the Trap.

I've been screaming and crying so much at the shelter. The staff wants to take me to a home because I go in and out of mental states. I walk to stores and coffee shops, and I don't see the people but all the dinners I used to have with the family and later Mrs. Eulalah. At the library, I don't see the screen but my mother talking to me, trying to convince herself that she didn't raise a monster.

Please, please, please believe me, I didn't have anything to do with him getting in the trap game. I haven't done anything since my stupid ass was sentenced six years ago. I'm going to miss you and everything you taught me about being a responsible man and not being a dickhead. I'm going to miss everything about Mrs. Eulalah's. I'm going to miss getting the boxes with Macalester every morning and start teaching me how to fight. I'm going to miss Nona pinching my cheek every time I got her a special iced coffee. I'm going to miss Aisha asking me my opinion about books even though I haven't read half of what she read. I'm going to miss all the human patterns of feeling the people in that shop and the people who came to that shop had, patterns that felt more normal than anything in my life.

Though you don't want to see me, I appreciate everything you did for my life, man. You took the time with me to get me in touch with my mama's sensitive book side. You and Estelle gave me a sense of standards that your dad didn't. I'm just so sorry I never got a chance to show you what that meant to me. I didn't do what y'all said I did this time, but I'm so sorry.

• • •

Oh, you want to talk to me about the incident? You want to find out the truth about what happened with me, Judith, and the professor? You want to find the truth and re-establish contact and shit? Or do you want to cover your daddy's ass —and by proxy your ass— because he really fucked up this time? Do you want to be buddies again? Or do you want to find something that I said that you can to pretzel to save his ass from the unsavable shit he did? Because he did some unsavable shit. It isn't like he hasn't done some unsavable shit before: Lord knows I wanted to kill the nigga when he put his hands on Estelle. But what kills me was that you were good with that, bro. You wanted "no canceling" and "community healing" with that. And now you're scared because he showed his crazy in front of a White woman. And you might get fired because you his boy. Well, kick rocks in flips flops, nigga. I saw the shit, and I hope Judith gets her bag. Kick rocks in flip-flops.

Notice my language change. Nigga. You ain't professor with me no more, dawg. If you gonna be a motherfucking shoeshine boy for Everett and shit, you is a nigga to me. This nigga whups more women than OJ and Ike combined, and your conscious ass is still trying to "cape" for him and find the truth. And don't give me no motherfucking game about "The People." I am fucking DONE with that shit. I got a small apartment in the old-ass Winthrop Hotel. I'm on aid. I can take my Black ass to the food bank. I don't need you, and you don't need to contact me for shit. Y'all broke me, motherfucker. Y'all broke me.

And you don't want to cancel me no more? And you found out your golf course Crip was lying to you? You mean to tell me OG triple OG food court curly fries got caught with another bag? With me nowhere in sight? And because the nigga don't know how to plea good, he got caught in a lie and had to admit that he put that shit in my pants and old spare room? And that Darren and James told him to put it there? And that I had nothing to do with no golf course trap? Wow! WOW! I wish you could see my not-shocked face. But you won't because I'm using that word you taught me, professor. BOUNDARIES. Don't fix your motherfucking mouth to say you're sorry. Don't even think of asking me to come back to that house and be a punching bag for y'all bougie-ass niggas.

As a matter of fact, for a final gift to you, I'll tell you the truth of what happened. The unvarnished truth, nigga, Would you like to know what the fuck I was doing there? Why I was back at the school in the first place? I didn't go there to start any shit with your punk-ass daddy. I went there to die. TO DIE. I went there to drown myself because it was where momma drowned herself. Processing losing everything was so motherfucking painful that the idea of drowning myself to death and apologizing to my mother face-to-face became alluring. If I couldn't get redemption, I could at least see her. I could at least apologize to her face. I could at least tell her I tried and that I had to bite it in this last act because I got off scot-free in the other ones.

I get off the bus, and I'm about to walk the tracks with the rocks in my jersey when I see Judith and your punk-ass daddy arguing over the class. They was going forward over the stupid-ass "Black Fire" art exhibit that just put a whole bunch of rocks in different shapes around a furnace in Red Square, and yes, I ran my ass over there.

"You need to stop following me, sir," she said, walking backward away from him.

"And you need to tell me you are not going to ruin my life. You were obnoxious, entitled, and now you are going to lynch me online because I didn't curtail my class to your needs." He grabbed her shoulder and I saw her freeze. I saw her freeze like everyone I used to stick up and those two old ladies I put my hands on.

"Take your hands off her, nigga, or I'll fuck you up."

"Fuck you, nigga," he screamed in the middle of Red Square. "You the biggest Uncle Tom I've seen in my life. Caping for this Jew girl who's gonna online-Trayvon me because I didn't curtail my class to her needs."

"Curtail class to my needs?" said Judith, pushing him off her. "First of all, what Damballa did to Jane Crow in Baraka's poem was a fraction of an inch from a lynching. And what the Flower Phantom did to Ishmael Reed's *Reckless Eyeballing* wasn't that fucking far off either. And second, I signed up for an intro to Black humanities class. I didn't sign up for a class to tell me why it should fucking be raped and murdered for the cause."

Just then, Judith noticed me disheveled and walked across to me. "Fuck man, are you okay?" And as soon as she did that, I could see his eyes flip to me and his hands start to raise.

"No. Let's just go, sis. Let's just find people." Judith used the moment to start walking next to me and we turned away from him.

"Nigga you ruined my family," Everett screamed while following us.

"Andre gave me the letter. I know your son was full of shit," I said to him over my shoulder.

"Listen, dude," she said to him, turning around to face him, "you're just going to have to deal with me, accept that I'm going to sue you, and stop following me."

"No, you are not going to ruin my life." he said, following us as we started to swerve past the "Black Fire" exhibit. "I've taken too much pain in this school and coming and going from this school. And I won't let that happen. And the coming revolution I am creating here won't let that happen."

"Do it, or I'll call the police on you."

"Call the police? Help! This karen is trying to kill me! This karen is trying to kill me!" some people start to turn to look at us, some of them recognized us.

"This nigga is full of shit!" I yelled out. "This nigga is full of shit!"

"You don't understand how a hateful life partner can do. You don't understand how a woman like that can bring a sensitive Black man to the edge," he said.

"Not my problem, dude," said Judith.

"Racism is your problem."

"You are my problem, you vile, ignorant, stereotypical, barbaric motherfucker."

And he grabbed her by her head and took her toward the fucking exhibit. I jump up on him, he elbows me, takes out a switchblade, and swings at me. I gave him a side tackle by the lake. He cut me up a little bit, and Judith took the knife and ran to the authorities. She got the police while he beat the dog shit out of me. But I took it. When the cops arrived they pull us apart, and get a few licks in on me too until Judith gets them to stop.

Because of his violence, they took me to a hospital where they got me a caseworker and an emergency Section 8 apartment. This is where I'll be, dawg. I have a good routine and ritual with these folks this month. Someday I will be able to talk with you again. But this is not the day. I can do bad myself, sir. Until then, kick rocks in flip-flops, nigga. You got a good hustle going, a golden ticket with all these police shootings, so people won't hold your ass to no standard. You'll probably keep your job, dawg. But ain't a goddamn thing happening between us. Kick rocks in flip-flops, nigga.

• • •

I'm so sorry I blew up on you and got paranoid at the food bank. I'm also sorry that circumstances dictated that we had to see each other again there. I just found out that you quit and broke down and are back on the block. Worse than that, I read the article that excoriated you for it. I just melted, man. Being excommunicated from the family is a fucking painful thing; I can tell you that firsthand. But to be roasted about it online? And to be told, you're not strong by some Black legacy dude, when you've been strong all your goddamn life? You told me what happened to you in these streets getting beat up and shit, and you told me what happened to your moms. I'm so sorry you had to go out like that.

I like to tell you that I ignore the blogs and the articles related to Everett and the Nisqually incident, but I can't. I have to though: I've been fighting the paranoia and the voices in my head for a while, and when I saw you I just saw the unrelenting stress of those years. Even though I don't feel bad about going off on Everett, I feel bad that I called you a nigga. You were such a good mentor and so nurturing to me, and I shouldn't have gone half-cocked at you, especially because you were in the same food bank line as me.

I'm trying to live a peaceful, quiet life away from Nisqually, but I'm going to testify for Judith next week. I have my routine: I take my daily sandwich I get from aid or the food bank, go to the library and read some of my momma's books, go home and act as a guard for the church ladies going in and out of the Winthrop Projects, go home and watch TV if there isn't a bingo night at the VFW down the street. Because I help the bingo ladies get home safe, a couple of the dope boys give me free weed. It's been the best pain medication for me, to be honest. I tried to go on the straight and narrow route, but the legal dope people in counseling put me on shit that makes my brain hurt. Their shit makes my brain do weird things and doesn't help. At least free weed makes me not faint and not think, and I really don't want to think.

I go to the library to get the past out of my head, Andre. I'm trying to write the book that makes her come back to me. I hear my momma's voice and see her cry so much. She isn't taunting me as much as I'm trying to acquire the skills that get everything in my life right with her, to hear her voice guide me like you say you hear your mother's.

I sometimes see Aisha and Macalester at the library, and it's a bit contentious. I had to yell at them to stop staring me down. I can't say enough times that I get why I got kicked out that joint, but I'm in the library at the free computer lab right now trying to live the rest of my life. There's no reason to reenact their disappointment and rage at me every time we cross paths, and I honestly wish they'd leave me alone. Reenacting disappointment and rage seems like a common theme in my life over the last year or two, so when I'm not on depressive spirals trying to find out about the Everett case, I keep my mind really light. Almost all YouTube funny clips.

At night I make the best of my basement life. From the bottom windows of the Winthrop Projects, the lights go in and out of the overworked power grid, jarring some neighbors, but keeping all but the most eager to visit away. I'm at the bottom of the old hotel turned tenements house, it was used as a storage room until the manager decided to give it to me for respite care, then Section 8 fees. I got a tidy arrangement aside from the lights. Built-in shower rods are nailed to a metal panel, and next to them is a makeshift record player and stereo next to his room. To the right side of the extensions are a small refrigerator and a portable heater, both on top of cinder blocks. In the center of the space is a table, a couch, four chairs and an old typewriter. It's a life, dawg, and I live it: I spend my days trying to become a better writer when I'm right and trying to forget the world when I'm wrong.

I hope that we can talk again someday, Andre. If I see you again, let's walk to the food bank. I heard you got a job at the bar, and I don't drink anymore, but I do some things at the library. I would love to see you there. We can talk about life and books in a way like we used to. Or at least go for a walk. I don't regret the best times that we had. I don't regret what I learned in college, especially my memories with Judith. I want to catch up with her again someday; it's that for all that social media and cultural stress at the school, she doesn't need me right now to add any more. I've just been too sick to go over there. I'll help you in these new streets if you help me process this. I still have a lot to process, man.

One more thing, man. I'm gonna give you some life game. Go home and say you are sorry to the shop. They love you, brother. They will take you back. Just dump the highbrow Hotep shit and start over. This is my gift to you, penance for years of being a fucknigga.

• • •

People were mad at my testimony, but I don't give a fuck. I have no illusions about Nisqually or my whole life there. I just took two buses past a rich White neighborhood and a richer White neighborhood. Then I took off at my stop and walked past the manufactured lake and tidy-ass meadow, passed Red Square and a bunch of screaming kids, up this castle-looking building till I got to where the Board of Regents were. Then they took me to an office that looked like a BET version of the courtroom in Al Pacino's *Scent of a Woman*. People have been taking depositions with a bunch of lawyers there, and it was my turn at bat. The school's lawyer had met me at the downtown library. We had had three sessions, so I was prepared for everything.

I just told them the truth, dawg. He swung at me, and I swung at him. He cut me up, but he didn't cut up Judith or take her to that fucking little furnace; I made sure of that. I don't give a fuck what he or any Blue Blood woke activist says on social media. That's what happened, and that's what I told them. After that, I took the bus past some more screaming-ass kids, past Red Square again, and past the manufactured lake and meadow to the bus stop where I took two more buses home to live the rest of my life.

That's it, dawg, the story about Wokelandia and me is over. I do not give a fuck if people on a blog are mad at me. I'm on the Block, just trying to live my life, trying to eat and write something coherent every day. I don't give a fuck if somebody doesn't like me on Facebook. I feel I'm doing more making sure women don't get robbed here than anything I was in school. What I'm doing feels completely honest, and it makes me happy. It's been one of the few times that I have been that way in my life.

And yes, Everett ever threw a fit. Yes, he was preaching to a bunch of kids like he was John the Baptist, but I didn't give a fuck. I —no, we— have heard that sermon before: he had bad hands handed to him in his, but he acts like he was the only nigga in the world who had bad hands handed to him. And we got to keep it 100; he dealt out more. And as much as I want to feel sorry for a lady who doesn't want me to call her aunt anymore, I can't get over the fact that she threw me away. I don't want anything bad to happen to her, but I don't want to hear how I sent her upper-middle-class twit into the Trap.

Coming into the apartment, I was in a good mood. The sun cleared up a bit, and it felt a little muggy (or at least muggy for Tacoma). They had some good meat at the Grocery Outlet, and the curry powder in the dollar section, so I'm going to the Winthrop in a really good mind-frame. I got my food cooking; I'm checking out my Sunkist powder from a diet soda, and I'm about to turn on sports radio to hear the lowdown on the Mariners when I hear a knock. I assume it's the super coming to complain about my radio again, and I tell him, "Yo, I got headphones yesterday. I'll take care of it."

"It ain't the super, baby," said Eulalah. I half-open the door to see her leaning on the windowsill.

"You can't kick me out of my apartment because you think I'm in the Trap."

"I'm sorry, baby. I know you're not."

"If you want me to give you a cookie for that, I'll give you a buck to go to the corner store. I'm cooking dinner right now."

"Kyle got caught."

"Again? Wowwwwwww. This is my shocked face. Can I finish my meat now?"

"Can I please sit down for a second? You lived in my basement enough times for free. Does that get me at least one sit-down?"

For five minutes, we didn't say anything: we looked back and forth at each other every 30 to 45 seconds as the Mariners pregame show went on. She and I tried to make small talk about the game, but we couldn't organize coherent sentences. After a while, I had to break the tension.

"How's Estelle?"

"I had to kick her out."

"You kicked her out before."

"This time, it's for real."

"I'll try to believe you."

"Ever since I cut off contact with you, almost everybody's been on my ass."

"No, they have not," I dropped my stirring fork onto the meat with a clatter.

"The fuck you mean 'No, they have not'?"

"Every time I see Aisha and Macalester in the library, they look down on me and scurry away as if they're ashamed to be in the same room."

"They're not ashamed of you; they're ashamed of me. And they're ashamed of themselves for following me."

Eulalah paused, took her toasted almond nails, put her hands to her face, then looked at me. "Albert, I was there when that little girl had nothing! She and your mama. Clinging on me not knowing they were, or how to put they head on a swivel. The carpet under the big screen? Right there, right there was the place they asked me to sleep at because they didn't want to go back to Hillside Terrace. You had a thug touch you? Albert, there isn't a goddamn woman who came up from these goddamn projects who don't have a goddamn story about men cruising or the uncle or they pappy wilding out trying to get at them. Every social scientist says 60-70% for us. And that included the burbs."

As I was about to say that I'd would never do shit like that, she held up a hand to keep me quiet. I looked up, bit my lip, and took a deep sigh.

"That's why I started this shop, and the shops downtown. I wanted to give them street girls a network, a leg up. Your mama and Estelle sat in that table, in my table, scouring for and learning grants so we could give street girls a good price and a good place. Street girls, all those girls these playas, deacons and internet niggas say are fast tailed. Twelve-year-old girls, Albert. And I wanted to give them something. I wanted to give them a life where they suffered less than me. And Estelle and your momma helped build it, that room, that room with their goddamned sweat. I saw you giving him money out front the shop and I started worrying before all that shit went down. And later you wanted me to give her word up for you because you wasn't a fuck up for eight months?

"But the worst thing, the worst thing," she said while taking her eyelashes off her welling eyes, "is that you were right. My day-ones and -twos tell me I've lost my mind. That it didn't make sense that you were in my basement and Estelle talking about you running a trap. My customers stopped coming. And Estelle starts to draw out the equity she can't cash. She turns so bad; she starts lecturing my customers are being ghetto and started proselytizing for that boy like Everett proselytized for his sad story. I know she's going through it, but she was as hard to deal with as your mama when she got sick. And Nona and Aisha just left. Nona decided to go back to counseling, and Aisha got enough scholarship money at UW to live there. Been so tense at the shop, they just sent to me by letter one morning. That was the last time I saw Estelle. I was sitting on the curb with Macalester, trying to figure out what the fuck I'm going to do with this shop when I saw her blue Lexus come in. Albert, I can still see how she walked to me, unnatural, too fast, her hands exaggerated. You could tell that she was disturbed if you paid attention.

" 'Girl, I got to tell you what they are saying about that thug Albert on the blogs,' she said.

" 'You going to come to rant again?' I asked her.

" 'Girl, you've known me for thirty years. I can come in here anytime.'

" 'The staff quit, Estelle.'

" 'What for? They want more money?'

" 'They quit because we ran out Albert, and your boy ain't shit.'

" 'Don't start with me. You know what he did to our family.'

" 'It don't make any damn sense, Estelle,' I tried to tell her, 'You've been trying to sell that this kid is a Kingpin when everybody knows how long he's been in my basement. I know what he did. I've got to know the women he did it to. I tried to believe you and be in your corner. And look what it got me.'

" 'What are you saying? Oh, you're throwing me away again,' she crossed her arms and turned away.

" 'I've had so many good memories of you, but I haven't had a good memory with you in years. The ladies in the chair call you Karen because that's what you act like here. You thumb your nose at us. Even before the scandal, you talk down to us. I'm tired of you. I'm so tired.'

" 'Okay, okay,' she started to hyperventilate and walk away.

"Just then, I wanted to go over there in a hug and say that I was sorry. She had the same sad look when she was a thirteen-year-old girl on the bus with your mama. She looked like a child who knew she had done something wrong. She whispered 'I'm sorry,' and I wanted to say it was okay. I wanted to pull up Chaka Khan's 'I Was Made To Love Him' from my record collection in the back and have a dance party like we used to. I just couldn't get past the lump in my throat. Before she got in her car, she said, 'I'm going to do some things. I'm gonna be somebody. I know I haven't made good on my potential, but the world isn't done with me yet,' and then drove away."

"So what now?"

"I got three other shops. You don't have to go to any of them. But find a way not to be a stranger."

"Okay."

"And throw that whack-ass meat in the garbage. I'm hungry. Let's go to the Southern Kitchen," she got up and tossed the jacket from the back of the chair to me.

"I'll save the meat. I'm on a budget."

"That's fair."

• • •

I've missed our meetings for bullshit reasons many a time, Dawg, but this ain't one of them. I knew I was gonna get a gun at the station when I got off the bus. I saw the aging men, little gang practice niggas of different generations, prodding a young nigga and looking straight at my ass as I was taking the 28 to you. Some memory told me his name was Keante, the little brother of some Crip I couldn't even remember anymore. They was pushing him, a slightly oblong boy who looked too much like me when I was eleven. They prodded him like they prodded me, just like now-faded men in gutters had once prodded them as boys. The specter of all our Big Thomases hung in the air.

The bus went past the station and up and down hills of apartments while the old boy and I fixated on each other. I looked back without being obvious about it; he was hyperventilating. I'd been him in this moment and knew his fidgeting was the gun safety going on and off. The bus crossed Division Street at the top of the hill, past blocks of aging houses in various states of consumption and disrepair. One by one people got off, leaving just us on 11th, right next to your bar. I got off, and with one eye I saw the old boy shadowing me. I took him the long way to your bar, past the windows of Leroy's corner store and Pacific Teriyaki, through the side street by the old laundry mat and the bar, until we were in the Walgreens parking lot, roughly back to where we started; just him and me and his little .38.

"St-st-stick," Keante put the gun in my back.

"Oh, aren't we just precious!" I said to him. I flinched as the boy's arm wavered with the piece, "look at me, cuz. I said look at me, cuz! I got this swatch, two sandwiches, and a bag full of books. Do I look like I got something for you to steal?"

I buckled at the sight of Keante's fingers shaking. Silver cars sped from a side street, pretending to be oblivious to us. Taking a step back from the boy, I dropped my backpack and put my hands up. "What you gonna do with that?"

"I... I'm gonna..."

"Gonna be what, nigga."

"I'm gonna be a Disciple, bitch."

"Disciples? Disciples? You want to be a Disciple? You thirteen, you stutter, and you can't look a motherfucker in the face when you point a gun at him. You don't get it, do you? Nigga, you are expendable. A vulnerable little nigga who got in a way of their operations."

"They said I can roll with them if I can run my gang."

"Run a gang?"

"They want me in."

"They want you in what?"

"Ini-"

"Sound it out."

"Ini-initatated."

"Initiation? That's why them old niggas sent you? Little nigga, the disciples didn't send you here to initiate you, they sent you so you would fuck up and get arrested. Niggas will look good getting rid of you."

As the boy started to hyperventilate, I took a step left to his face, "and please tell me, lil cuz, what you gonna do with this? Just tell me what you gonna do with it, Keante? You gonna trade this for a brick? Streets really calling for a hot-ass copy of Lucille Clifton, nigga?"

"Give... Give... gimme your loot, nigga. Gimme your loot."

"Why am I not scared of you right now? I know you stupid, but why am I not scared of you? You got a gun on me, and I'm not shaking in my motherfucking boots. Why?"

"Quit talking, nigga! Quick talking or I'll bus' a cap in–"

"The safety off. Take the safety off, Keante. Do you know how to do it? Here, let me show you," and I pulled the gun from his hand gentle, like he was handing me a kitten, "and now I have the gun."

The boy broke into tears while I sat him on the curb. "Stop crying, cuz. I said stop crying and sit your punk ass down. I ain't gonna shoot you." I grabbed a drink and a tissue he had in the back pocket of his backpack, then firmly put my left hand around his shoulder, flicking the safety on the gun with my right.

"Normally with niggas who try to rob me, I would give them a street sense lecture about who to rob. I'd tell them, 'take a look all around here. See those people coming in and out of those apartments to get some cocaine.' I would say, 'They have expendable income and no recourse to snitch on you because they can't be telling the police that somebody took their money for blow.' And I would end it by saying, 'But do you go rob them? Nooo, you got to come fuck with me. Even for a criminal, you a simple bastard.' But I can't say that with you can I?"

"...no."

"You ain't in no gang."

"I wanna be. I'm gonna be."

"You in your little young'un' practice crew of niggas who got turned out by Crips. Like I used to be."

"...yes."

"And they send you because they recognized me and saw me doing good and got mad."

"Yes."

"You can cry now." I looked him over, "when did they get you?"

"Twelve?"

"How old are you now?"

"Seventeen."

"Take this $20 and my walking shorts from my backpack. Tell them you robbed me and gave me a Huey Newton job with a tree branch behind the Walgreens."

Right after he nodded, the cops came and we both had run off, me with a gun in my hand, the old boy with charges I didn't know but sadly knew.

Yeah Andre, I've missed our meetings for bullshit reasons many a time, Dawg, but this ain't one of 'em.

• • •

It's been great talking with you regularly again. Next time, can we talk about how overwhelmed I am by some shit? Life is going faster than I can fathom right now. Remember that *American Masters* episode of F. Scott Fitzgerald, where he's talking about *This Side of Paradise* being a smash hit, and him talking about something like having an unbelievable mixture of joy and terror and mania in his brain? I kind of feel that right now. No, I really feel that shit right now.

So it was Sunday, and I was waiting for the Winthrop sisters to get off the bus stop on the 28th like I usually do. I was walking past the new hipster food market they put on Commerce. Andre, I don't pay it any mind: the White folks are harmless; the neighborhoods are changing a little bit, but I don't hate it as much as I hated my time in Nisqually. So I'm walking with the church ladies, asking him about how the service was, listening to their linked conversations about who's messing around and who drop-kicked who, and carrying on like it's a normal-ass Sunday. And I hear her voice.

"Albert... Albert!"

I almost recognized it in the crowd, then I heard it again, just behind me.

"Albert."

And it was Judith. And it made me feel manically joyful in a certain way that they didn't feel manic before. Maybe because it was outside of Nisqually, and she sounded relaxed. But I didn't realize how much I missed in form and content; I missed hearing it and feeling the world made a little more sense than before. "It's really good to see you. I got to take the sisters back to the apartments, but we should meet up."

"Can you come back downstairs, and we can talk at Tully's?"

"Sure," I said, "give me twenty minutes."

I made sure everybody got home safely, put on my dollar store suit and walked down to the coffee shop. You know the Tully's that used to be an old antique place where crackheads hung out? I walk in there, we hug, I get an iced mocha, and we sit at the table that sticks out with all the windows to catch up. "Have you been able to get to another school, or get some peace with Nisqually?" I asked.

"Oh, dear fucking God, no. It's been hell. I've gotten harassed almost every day for months by people who think I'm a racist for taking down an influential Black man. I've lost count of the conspiracy kooks telling me that I am a false flag. I hear all kind of stories about how he was hugging me to get me to stop, how I didn't get his love language, how he was trying to hold me sturdy to get me to be quiet, and I leaned into his arms, and how he didn't really drag me toward the 'Black Fire' furnace in the middle of the art exhibit. I had to move with the settlement money, I got a house by Titlow Bay because of the constant stream of people who tell me I am a monster to my face. It's going to worsen because he's suing the school for discrimination for all the stuff he's taken over the past twenty years."

"I'm so sorry."

"I can't go much of anywhere. I just go to the store and the coffee shop outside of my house. If I go to any liberal place, people will start saying that I am the enemy of social justice and have a hard time dealing with it. I just don't have that many people to talk to."

"Well, here's my email and phone number. I'll meet you when or wherever you want. Feel free to talk to me anytime or get coffee when you want to escape."

"Yay! How is your life? Are you okay here?"

"I'm pretty much okay. I protect the sisters on the block going to bingo and going to the store. When I feel healthy, I go to the library and read there. I do my best to avoid the internet, but..." I trail off, taking a sip of my coffee.

"The case is in the papers, and sometimes it's hard to avoid that, and when you see it, you go into a spiral..."

"Exactly!"

"It's too painful."

"Dear God, yeah."

"And I can't fucking go to my brothers to talk about it. They're so fucking far down the Proud Boy rabbit hole; the group got them pulling out White replacement stickers and throwing milkshakes from cars at anybody who doesn't look like them. And when I try to tell them there's a different way, they just point to Nisqually. And when I tell them the world isn't Nisqually, that there's a truth in the middle and that the middle doesn't skewer to a dead median when it comes to American history, they just point to Nisqually and tell me I'm a masochist. And that I left them..." She stopped a second. I could tell that hit home with her, even if it was bullshit.

"Oh, my friend, my friend. You didn't leave them." I patted her hand. She spread her palm flat and let mine rest on hers.

"I swear to God, Albert, I tell them that. Try to say to them that I couldn't get hit in the head anymore and I couldn't live in that much fear. Yes, he could be kind and tender when he wasn't drunk. Yes, he saw too much in his tours in Iraq and Libya. Yes, yes, he was in perpetual grief over losing his wife and an upbringing in Russia I couldn't fucking fathom. But I was dying, man. Every day felt like death. Richard Noland was the counselor at Olympic Junior High, and he tried to help us for several years. And when he saw me down ten pounds after a junior high debate match, he adopted me and took me with him when he went to Tacoma. Richard gave me family stability and the ability to see the world outside of my father's drunken agony-sphere." She leaned back, pulling her hand out from under mine. I left mine where it was and hoped she didn't notice my being awkward.

"I had to leave, but I didn't leave them. But I can't tell them that, Albert, they're more mad at me than they are at my father. And I'm so alone. I feel so alone. The settlement has been good to me, but I feel so alone, Albert."

I tried to process my feelings because of what you said about friendship because I appreciated her friendship and the boundaries set there. In your own ways, you both taught me how to be a man about that shit. To embrace the meaning of friendship. To not be a boy trying to mack. But she reached out and grabbed my hand this time, and I couldn't say anything. She nodded to the bill and put a card in, and we walked to the counter, not even looking at the lady behind it.

We walked outside, and she pulled me close. And then she kissed me. And everything after that was a blur of emotions and feelings. I remember walking backwards past the door to the Winthrop, then going to the elevator, then going to my room, and then hairs and synapses, and the way her skin felt on mine, colors in the deepest feeling of joy ever felt in my life, and then feeling that I didn't deserve this joy. About the time I became coherent, she was cooking me eggs and telling me that she wasn't leaving here without me, and she didn't.

Everything is overwhelming. Everything is joyful. Everything is terrifying.

• • •

I am in delirium. This is like crack but I don't feel twisted. I love Judith more than anything in the fucking world. We go out of town and up and around the state and I feel like my feet are off the ground.

When we get out of Wokelandia we are the most adorable young hipster nerds on the planet. We get away to vacations in these hotels where we smoke out the room and eat the dopest room service. And when we ain't fucking or fucked up, we go out and put on plaid and beanie caps and cool-ass scarves and shit and become different, freer people. The same people, but different and freer in a way.

Man, she got a brother going to brunch in Ballard, putting quinoa, raspberry vinaigrette, and baked chicken in wraps. Baked chicken is the Solange of foods. Yeah, it ain't Beyonce. But that don't mean it isn't something special. I be sitting with these twee kids and White ladies with big-ass hats having conversations and it doesn't seem like hell on earth, man. And nobody bombards us for "taking a great Black man down."

I swear to God, dawg, the first time she got deep into my heart wasn't sex. Don't get me wrong, Andre, sex felt great and wonderful. But it was one time she held me during the *British Bake Off* show. No bullshit, just holding.

Straight up Luther intimacy cuddling shit. It was when this heavyset brother was self-conscious about his cake and started looking down from the camera with these sad terrier eyes, and everybody came around him to say it was okay, he was doing a good job, and was trying to help them. That moment, Andre, that moment was so endearing that we just hugged right there in the bed. I was just gonna go to the store and buy breakfast and she told me to look at that moment and we just sat there and hugged. And it felt great. She tells me that it isn't impossible to work through times Big Thomas ran through me. That I can heal if I work through it. Not ignore it, but work through it.

I'll do anything in the world to make her happy. The world stops when she smiles because it's come from the soul of someone who deserves them more than anybody I know. And when I do shit to make her smile the world feels more right in its axis than any time in this world.

It was really beautiful to have a reunion of the shop at the coffeehouse. They really light up when you're around because you don't have my bullshit. You are their fave and deservedly so. I'm so happy Macalester has a self defense class at the Rainbow Place and Aisha is doing so good in school. And I don't know what's going on with you and Nona, but I like it. I'm a rookie in this relationship game, but I know chemistry, and you two got it.

How are we really dealing with the daily political shit, man? We got this nice two-story two blocks down the hill from the water. The nice old White neighbors leave us alone and once a week we play pinochle at Barb's house at the bottom of the hill (we got old liberal swag on lock). We know there is a movement for Scott at the school. We just don't care anymore because we are still on boyfriend/girlfriend island. I know you are worried about our mental state and how we've become stoners, but we're fine. We get high and fuck a lot, and we just want to make each other happy. We're comfortable, have all our needs met, have more than enough money, and love each other deliriously. That's all that matters to me right now.

When I say I don't want to talk about the articles, that doesn't mean I don't know that they exist. I know every article that phrased and twisted what happened in a fucked-up way. The Assata Shakur Foundation in Portland accused Judith of trying to kill the professor when she threatened to call the police on him for stalking her? Check. Evergreen State's African Collective's YouTube podcast said she was a racist for calling him ignorant? Check? Nisqually's student paper wrote a thousand goddamn words about how ignorant she was for calling him a barbaric motherfucker, given his history in the community? All of these motherfuckers getting between four to six figures worth of clicks on Facebook and Twitter? Check. I can't do anything about them or change their minds. I can only make one woman happy, and I'm going to keep doing that.

• • •

Andre

So you telling me you back, Nona is back, Aisha's back for winter break, and you wanna do good for the shop? Then let me give you the new instillation of the game at Eulalah's:

If you are there in the morning before Macalester, make sure you wash her headscarves. Replace them if they get bad. Do this without her knowing. Macalester loves to get the Diana Ross *Mahogany* 1975 scarf they sell at the Saturday swap meet at the B&I, but she has a Marsha Warfield/Babyface flat top perm that fades them out quick. Put a Berkeley mint in her Patti Labelle caftans and say they came from Black Trans Jesus. Do not be surprised if she asks you about the game (trust me, brush up on your ESPN).

If Eulalah gets a little wavy with the Crown Royal, tell her to drink Perrier because it's good for her skin and Joe Louis drank it (and make sure to get the bottles of Perrier, because when she holds the bottles she thinks of the pictures of Joe Louis drinking Perrier at her grandparent's and they were the only people to love her as a child). When Nona and Aisha come in, have an ice caramel frappe and a single shot mocha for them respectively, with a small little flask of Seagrams to put in it if Nona is in a mood.

A skinny little boy named Ledarius will come in to try and sell pillows he stole from his homophobic uncle at the swap meet. He interrupts when it is busy, but he means well and he listens, so navigate a time for him to trade his shit. The rest I ain't got to tell you. I know you are on #teamnona and Nona is on #teamyou, just lean on what you know, learn on the go, and know when to shut the fuck up.

I'll be back someday. They love you. They will be so happy with you. They will be happier with you than they were with me. I got debts, man, and I still die a little each time thinking about them. I know I shouldn't. I got a wonderful woman and I know the shop loves me. But debts don't work like that. Not the ones you can't pay.

• • •

I'm so sorry we were high when you and the shop came over to visit us at the house. We've been going through a tough time.

So we're dabbing and we lose track of a day or two when I decide to sober up and make some food. I drink a half gallon of water, put a pour on, turn on the radio, flip some channels and hear this.

"This is Benjamin Izeola for *Minority Concerns*: the show for Black life that matters. In the early to mid '90s, Dr. Scott Everett became the most well-known writer from Tacoma with *Division Fork*, his bestselling autobiographical novel. Everett has been a figure of controversy in recent years, most notably in relation to his recent dismissal from Nisqually University over charges of sexism, antisemitism, and domestic violence. But now, with his upcoming lawsuit against Nisqually and his book being reissued by Mercer Island's brand new American Criminal press, he has resurfaced as a figure of notoriety in Northwest academia and the African American Community.

"Published in October 1992, *Fork* was Everett's autobiographical tale of busing from Tacoma to University Place, and his life as a college student in Nisqually. Often compared to Chester Himes and John

Williams, it is a book that is now considered a modern classic of Northwest literature. It spent three weeks in the New York Times Best Seller list and made him one of the leading spokespeople on race to this day. Dr. Everett, you were a civil rights figure yourself, how do you square that with this recent spat of accusations?"

"Yes, I made my mistakes. But I made my mistakes as a man. I set a blueprint where no other Black man went and I am not a saint. But I have done too much to be thrown away by the system. I've done too much good for my people and have gone through hell doing it. I am *owed. I went through so much agony to make this area better.* And the people who did this to me need to pay. Nisqually, the literary system–"

And I turned the radio off because I knew we were going to be the next thing he mentioned. And I saw Judith looking at the radio so desolate, and we just made love and smoked weed until you and the salon came in the house and saw us high off our ass the next morning.

We're going to get our shit together. We just got to get her brothers right and out the Proud Boys, then go somewhere that won't torture us for not being woke or being a nigga and a Jew who like to fuck and get high. Please don't give up on us. I'm gonna get the strength to go back to the shop again. I know there's something wrong with me and saying that because I understand why she believed Estelle deep down inside. One of the reasons that I'm glad we still talk. I know you're a bartender now, but you got nothing to be ashamed of in regard to the psychology degree you got at Nisqually. You helped me so much. I'm also glad that you're there more often and part of that family.

• • •

It was so dope to go out to dinner with you and Nona. Y'all are ridiculously cute together. We can't go out as much as we used to because of how Scott branded us; the last three times we went to eat we got accosted by people who wanted to perform on Black Twitter or turn us into a TikTok. So it was great to have good company. Also, don't worry that you talked about him too much, dawg. Everett was your father and you are going to testify against him in his bullshit trial. I know —or at least I think I know— a thing or two about becoming a different person.

I think if you break it to Eulalah gentle, she'll understand Nona's need to go back to school. Nothing lasts forever and she knows that. I've seen her deliver sermons on not letting the shop go, followed by her admitting she needs to find somebody. To love her is to know her tics, I ain't got to tell you shit about that.

The next time we talk, I got to tell you when I saw Estelle last. After our get-together, we went to the Grand to watch a Sidney Lumet film festival and were kind of in our haze of an intellectual debate about whether or not *The Fugitive Kind* worked as a movie. She was like "it was a grand, aesthetically extravagant failure that helped him write such Minimalist masterpieces as *Dog Day Afternoon* and *The Verdict*." My take on it was that even though it was too motherfucking long, there was too much of it that was magical. Call it a failure, but grade B Tennessee Williams material is still better than so many other people's pen game. We were wrapped in this conversation from the theater back through Whole Foods when I saw Estelle looking at me as I was picking wine.

I nod and I walk away, and she keeps following me. So much so that I'm just going past aisles not to get food but to hide from her. Judith and I get to the line, and she's behind us. And after we pay, I say as respectfully as possible, "would you please leave us alone? I respect why you chose to believe who you chose to believe, but you are putting your anger on us and around us for far too long. I'm not responsible for your decisions. I'm not responsible for the life you fucked up. Eulalah is not responsible for the life you fucked up."

We walked briskly to the car, trying to forget her when her scream stopped us. "Can I be your friend?" she cried. "I miss friends. I'm sorry I thought you were a drug dealer again."

I turned around and looked at her. "Everybody hates me," she said. "Suburban White folks think I raised a trap man and he's why Trump got elected or should have. Black folks here think I'm the reason their beauty shop closed. My husband has no time for me as a person. My son is doing time for drug possession. All these college student activists come in and out of my house and treat me like I'm the maid.

"And worst of all, Eulalah won't talk to me. I know I made mistakes. But ever since I got with Everett, all that shop has seen in me is a person who lived in a house in University Place. It didn't matter that a year-and-a-half before I lived in the Hillside Terrace housing projects. I have no friends, Albert. I only want a friend. Can you be my friend?"

And I wanted to say yes, and hug her, but felt that same wall in my throat that Eulalah talked about. I closed the door and tried to start the car before I began to cry.

• • •

I guess you heard about the gun incident, dawg. What the motherfuckers talking about it on the net don't say is that they found him. That him. Fuck, man, they found his ass. I want to stay high until I die right now.

It was the first winter day that wasn't cold, and I realized that we hadn't talked in a while, so I was gonna hit you up today regardless. It was late morning, and no protesters showed up, so I thought that was a good sign. Judith felt groggy from drinking too much the night before, so I took the Lexus up the street to get some cheese and meat croissants to soak that shit. I came back, and there the crowd was, and there he was. I was surprised to see him, and then I wasn't. I was surprised he had a swap meet dashiki, and then I wasn't. He had grown an afro and was telling his prison nigga story, and I was more surprised that only half the anarchists were listening. When I got out of the car, he gave me that same stare and smile when he used to corner me by the Ainsworth Quick-E-Mart and demand that I get money for him or suck his dick.

"Bruh, the revolution can save all of us," he said as I put my right hand on my face while walking by him.

"Thomas, go to hell and wait till I see you," I said, walking past him. I hoped for a split that he wouldn't recognize me, but he did.

"You don't understand the wonder of it, cuz. In the joint, I thought I wasn't shit for doing what I did to you. I thought I wasn't shit for banging and running the Trap. But then these folks came and was telling me that this shit wasn't on me. The Northwest Black Liberation Front and the Puget Sound Anarchists."

"Come off that shit."

"No, bro. Listen. List-en. They schooled me on my own history. They schooled me on my own struggle and how it's tied to other struggles. They told me I'm a product of a hundred years of oppression, and the Project Industrial Complex."

"Nigga, come off that shit. You wanna come to my house talking all this jive-ass prison intellectual shit? Why don't you read something about a block that wasn't a northern ghetto? Maybe you'll see we had it better than most niggas on blocks. Take responsibility for your shit. You needed Reagan's Cuban Trap Fuckups dumping dope on the block more than Reagan did, nigga."

"Naw, nigga. Naw, nigga," he rushed me like he used to rush me when I told him no. He stopped a foot short, looked quick to the right of me, and raised his hands. I turned to see Judith with a .38.

"Yo, lady... lady," said Thomas, as the college kids started to back up.

"I thought you anarchists liked violence."

"Lady, please," he said, backing up to the fence as the protestors got in their Acuras and Genesises. "You don't understand. This is greater than us or me. God called me, the God of Black Liberation called me to be a leader and a witness for the greater good. God called me to lead my gangbanger partners and little soldiers in and out the joint."

"Your God ain't shit."

"Don't curse God. Don't curse God, my nigga. He has a plan for me. He has a plan to turn my street soldiers into soldiers for the cause against the capitalist pigs."

"Come off it, nigga."

"You don't understand," he said, backing away with his hands in prayer or in pleading, "this is for the greater good. I'm gonna be an activist and save the people for the greater good because of God's law. It's not my law. It's not your law. It's God's law, my nigga. You have to forgive me. You have to forgive me."

With that, Judith took me inside, and we crawled around a dab pipe. And we been there ever since. I want to stay high, dawg. And to keep it a buck with you, you asking me about it is asking too much from me. I know I get short with you when you have been talking to me about Big Thomas recently, but you told me to suck it up when I first saw you, remember? Don't get religion about how fucked up it is now. I deal the way I want to deal with him, and I'm a constructive citizen. Don't get religion on how fucked up Big Thomas was now.

• • •

Andre, I promise we will talk soon because the world is fucking caving in on us. I know we're not living right and living too fast; everything makes us tired, so tired.

Everett had a friend who brought up "receipts" to some of the shit he went through, and people have lost their motherfucking minds around us. I don't know what he did to get these motherfuckers to develop a conscience, but he did. And now Everett has the entire social justice world in the Northwest wrapped up in his sad story. How do we know this? The motherfuckers show up at the house to harass us every day.

And yes, I know the tales; the board members regularly called him a boy? They told jokes about how he wrote a novel while not being able to read? They underpaid him, badgered him for his syllabi for twenty years, back when he had decent syllabi, and excluded him from meetings that he should have been involved in? Professor, I heard it so much of them, I could finish his fucking stories. But the rest of the world hasn't, and the nigga is going to get his bag. The fucked up thing is all these immature kids are conflating what happened to him with what he did to us, or harassing us like that society's child shit you preached against.

To top all of that off, we had a day from hell yesterday. Three days before, Judith gets a call from jail from her two brothers telling her they got caught up in a meth beef. We go to the same building and the same fucking courtroom where I saw my mother last, with the same judge, and sit in the same back pew where she sat when she told me off. I'm holding Judith's hand, trying to support her and trying not have a stroke from my own memories. The deja vu keeps hammering me when the same exact heavyset cop who dragged my mama out all those years ago sits down and starts whispering to me; "these Proud Boys are worse than the hoppers running the streets, at least they know to keep it in the hood. This shit shows no respect for real citizens, am I right, buddy?"

I knew the game; he saw my clean threads and thought I was here to see some White boys suffer. I knew this cop would be spitting the most racist shit to me right now if I was White and it was a Black man in the docket; and he wouldn't be about any buddy shit if he recognized it was me in that box a few years back.

I looked at him in silence, then back at Judith when she grabbed tightly onto my arm. Her two brothers were being brought in wearing yardbird orange and shackles, but with defiant smirks on their faces. We looked at each other; stricken faces upon stricken faces that could just watch shit go down.

And it did go down. Those two scruffy-ass wanna-be Proud Boys posers got hung to dry, dawg. I tried to feel sorry for them before, tried to reach them because I loved Judith, but they were so deep in that Proud Boy shit. Apparently so deep that they got set up for drugs. I told those motherfuckers when they called the house they didn't know the hustle they were in. Every gang finds a fucking avenue to make the weakest link take the fall. And that's exactly what the fuck happened. Those boys are kingpins only as much as I was a kingpin, but both distributors and runners from the sticks had snitched on them, and there were just too many people willing to testify for them not to plead to five to dodge fifty. They had sneered at Judith and me before the sentencing, but after those five years per charge / four charge sentence numbers ran concurrent, they looked at me and Judith like two little lost baby birds. And for a second I thought I was looking at two versions of myself. I could see the moment in their minds when their horns grew and their pupils started to see everything in shades of red and black. The bailiff took them away, and that same cop, befuddled at my stricken face, had to escort our weeping asses to the coffee shop in front of the courtroom.

• • •

We tried to go to the brunch place up that hill street next to the library to get our minds off what just happened. But as soon as we sat down and started to exhale, guess what? You know Nick Oscar, the former fake trap rapper who bragged about not voting, then got all that money with his failed mayoral candidacy? The one you and Nona were going off about the last time we were at the coffee shop? Well, Murphy and all of his Laws showed up on our ass because the nigga picked the place to restart his brunch protests. A bunch a niggas in swap meet dashikis screaming, "fuck your brunch. The revolution is here to make you uncomfortable." And before I motherfucking know it, two of his goons see us and start to relitigate our issues with Everett. I swung at the dude, and she had to drag me out for my safety. We decided to go home to spend the next four to five hours doing dabs and having sex to take care of ourselves.

The problem was that, while sobering up before court, we had reached out to find my grandaddy across the bridge in Gig Harbor. I have this pleasant conversation with them, and scheduled this dinner with me and Judith; something we would have forgot if we didn't put it in our laptop planners like the responsible-ass adults we wanted to be. So we hear the beep and see the shit and try and sober up as fast as we could. We take a shower, dress fast, and walk briskly to the fish house where we were supposed to meet.

And just as we turn to the fish house, I saw the PCP funk man just like my mother and Eulalah described him, only heavier and wider, and a waist that showed that he was wearing a diaper. He was surrounded by these two short old Black folks who would have looked like the most adorable couple if they weren't bickering. And as I thought that, I got mad at myself for thinking they were adorable. Why couldn't they help me when I was a boy? Why couldn't they help my mama? They had enough money to live in Gig Harbor, so why didn't my mother receive a dime in child support? Why couldn't we have been a blended family, or would we have been the signs of poverty to their neighbors?

"We can never have a good day, Ethel," the man said.

"How many times I have to tell you, Andrew, our boy isn't normal," she replied, "our boy will never be normal again. And our lives will be peaceful when we understand that and start the process of putting him in a home."

"I can't, Ethel. I can't. I can't. I can't. I can't."

He looked like a lot of sherm heads I saw who couldn't deal with the noise in their brains fried with formaldehyde and whatever else they could get their findin'-ass hands on. You could almost overlook the fresh drool on his black dress suit and tie and the black pants that had the outside print of a diaper. I saw the clock was nine and a swarm of cars coming and realized we had made a mistake. Nisqually Prep was in a playoff game that just ended, and kids and their parents were starting to come into town. The boys outside started to laugh at him, and the old man —no, let me be specific— my grandfather took his pants off, exposed his overflow, and looked as if he was having a panic attack. That's when he spotted me, looked me up and down, looked to Ethel to mouth the world "Yeah, he's Joshua's", only to have her point at my father on the ground.

Judith and I ran in, and I took my father's pants off the way I used to take the pants off elders at bingo night who are incontinent. Judith found a hose and gently sprayed his bottom, then sprayed the fecal matter past the parking lot and into the rocks leading to the train tracks. My grandfather took one of his spare pants from the trunk and tried to put them on my zonked out father, struggling with his bulk. "I can't thank you enough... grandson," he said as I lifted my father's legs for him to slip the pants over.

"You're welcome, sir."

In the middle of the Fish House parking lot, my grandfather struggled to say something, then looked at my grandmother, leaning on the side of the car trunk with her hair down. He and I took my father with his clean pants to the car and put him in the back seat. My grandpa closed the door, looked me in the eye, tried to extend his left hand, then started to cry.

• • •

Fuck all you trying to get into our lives with this concern shit. You niggas need to stop talking about my drug addiction and stop talking about me. Stop talking about everybody wants to help us. We're in pain, and nobody cares about us. Yet everybody, everybody is showing up at our door for some bullshit.

We're in a motherfucking pandemic and George Floyd getting shot got these motherfucking prep school kids so brave they're showing up around the house, talking about how we're the enemy of the people and need to be shamed. I don't give a fuck if the numbers are going down and almost all of them have masks. They show up around the house looking like trust fund anarchists, and I'm sick of all them. We just want to live the rest of our lives doing what we want, and the only thing we want is get high, fuck, and die.

And stop complaining that we got tinfoil around our doors. They're our doors, motherfucker. And don't dare fix your mouth to complain that I brandished a shotgun when Darren got in my yard. I don't trust the motherfucker. I came off a bender one evening, and he's talking about changing as a man and feeling sorry and forgiveness and being confused about how cruel politics are. Talking about he didn't want to post the video out but he was scared Scott was gonna cut him off. Talking about how sorry he was for setting me up and that he didn't have a daddy and thought Everett was their daddy until he called him bitch the first time he told him no. You niggas need better daddy radar.

I was one of the dumbest little street niggas to come down the pike and I didn't see him as a father, even when he was an Obama nigga. So yeah, I chased that nigga off with a shotgun, and nigga if you show up on me and Judith's yard and I'll run you out too, motherfucker. All y'all talking about how you didn't know about some of the bullshit about Everett and feel lost as men. Fuck that shit. I'm done with that shit in my heart. They beat the brakes off me and bullied the fuck out of us in class, now he wants me to forgive him? Fuck that and fuck them.

And fuck you too, you stiff motherfucker. I hate you, I hate you, I hate you motherfucker. Concern-trolling about our drug use instead of all these motherfuckers around the house. Stay out our business. I don't trust you no more. I don't believe you. You're tied into this shit, aren't you? You want to get back with yo' daddy. You got that settlement money he wants to make a hustle out of George Floyd. I know that. I know that. You want to get that George Floyd money, don't you? You want to get that BLM hustle money, don't you? You scamming. You a motherfucking grifter. You went against everything you believe in. Get out of my life, dawg. Let us do whatever the fuck we want for the rest of our lives. We smoke crack, this what we want to do, and stay out our business or you will get this business end, motherfucker.

• • •

I'm so sorry we're sick. I'm so sorry Judith pulled a gun on you and the shop for trying to save us. It's my fault, man. It's my fault. I started all this.

I really appreciate you getting the group together to get us all in rehab. Even Estelle. Me and her been sick for so long. I wish you hadn't seen the trash bags and the shit on the walls. I'm gonna burn in hell for what I did to break my mother and for what I said to you. I'm so sorry we made Nona, Aisha, and Macalester cry when Judith pulled the gun. I would have gone with y'all, but I've been sick. I've been really ill, and I can't leave her because I started this. I caused this pain.

She's sick, man. She's really sick. She talks to walls, talks to her dad all day and in fucked up tongues. She could deal with the dabs but when we smoked that glass we lost our shit. And after she pulled that gun to get you out of the house, she turned the gun on me. Ever since I made the mistake of calling her Judy instead of Judith. We weren't arguing. We were eating those jelly beans Nona and Macalester left (we didn't have any food around the place anymore), and not really awake. I said "Judy, we need to get healthy." I just had cottonmouth and wasn't thinking. I didn't mean to talk about her size. I meant to say we should stop smoking crack and meth. But she lost it and I lost her. Oh my God, I have never felt so much pain in the world outside of my mother. She said I didn't love her. I love her more than anything in the world. And she said I didn't love her. She taught me how to love, and she said I didn't love her. I made her sick. I made her so sick when I called her Big Booty Jewdy when she was in such a tortured state as a high schooler. I understand why she doesn't trust me. I understand why no one trusts me. I don't deserve it. I don't deserve it. I beg God to kill me every day. I'm a horrible person. I'm a horrible person.

• • •

I'm going to fix everything.

I started all of this when my horns grew. I am the dragon and the fire that has tormented everyone's imaginations. I will end all of it, sir. It will all end with me.

Last night I came off a jag and I saw Judith on the floor. She was writhing and bouncing and praying to God to end her pain. I cradled her and took her to bed as she kept calling on Yahweh, Jesus, Buddha, and Allah to end her sorrow, to end these visions of her father, brothers, and my fucked-up self. I'm not even sure if she knew I was really there. I laid her on our bed and sat at the end of the bedroom and prayed with her, hoping it would give her calm. I sang her the gospel songs Estelle and Nona would sing to me when I started to cry about my mother. "I'm Leaning on The Everlasting Arms." "I'm On My Way to Canaan Land." "Oh, Mary Don't You Weep, Don't You Moan", and I look up and I ask God to repeat Mary's miracle. I asked the Black Jesus on Eulalah's wall to show up at the door and imagined where I point at his Black afro and say, "if you had been here, she wouldn't be suffering," and he would say, "for the benefit of your niggas who don't believe," and point to a spot where she would be there healthy and healed. I saw her in the light with white robes. And I would tell her I love her. I would go toward her and touch her forehead, "let me bring you water, love. Let me bring you a little water."

I wake up in the blue dawn and she's smoking again. So I made the decision.

I will make the water right.

I will set everybody free.

Yes, today is the day I will see her again. I see the light as I write you, dawg. I will raise and walk from the fire ants burning my body. I will walk the spitting flames of the voices in my head. I will walk through the fire pit and the frat house. I will not slip past the blood as I run to the rocks by the water. I will raze the hiding places and tear down the walls and binds of sorrow I built for all of you. Then. Then I will look at her in all the shades of blue and beg for mercy. I will tell her I tried but couldn't outrun my sins. I will fall down on my knees at the water basin and pray to whatever religion will forgive me. I hope you will forgive me someday.

I hope Estelle, Mrs. Eulalah, Nona, and Aisha can forgive me. I hope and hope Judith can forgive me. I hope they know I am setting them free because there's no more Monster to ruin their lives. I will re-baptize my body in the medium of the Sound. I will be both Beowulf and Grendel to make sure no one else gets hurt. *My bloodletting days are finished. I am a thug. Robber. Abuser. Destroyer. I am the link in all darkness. The talons in y'all's night. My life is pain and chaos and sorrow. I'm not Grendel. I'm worst than that nigga. And I will make everything right by the water.*

• • •

Dear Albert,

I'm not good at exits, young brother, and you have made me do more of them than anyone on this planet. But I have to write you this goodbye now.

The first thing your death forced me to do was say goodbye to my own mama. I swear to God, young brother, I didn't understand you because I was such a mama's boy. Ann Thompson was my affixed North Star. On everything I love, I'd give fingers and thumbs to have more days with her. And when you showed up, I saw a nigga who punked his mama to her grave. I had gone to school from the exact same Winthrop you lived; my Aunt Helen would teach and my mama would get money part-time from Mrs. Eulalah. And when she broke and jumped out the window when SSI chased her for her side money, followed by my aunt dying of a heart attack, Eulalah and the shop were the only things that kept me alive.

So I didn't know how to deal with you. My faith in Everett started to crack when you showed up smiling in those manhood confessionals I once thought were half candor and half cry for help. And after Estelle and Scott had that summit, I went to Eulalah myself and told her if you fuck up, I'd pistol whip you in the parking lot and have her tell the cops you jumped me. But you didn't fuck up. You grew. And I grew. And the shop grew to love you before Scott shrunk. No; rotted. A decay whose extensions broke us in the shop us and sent you to the water.

There I go again, dammit, making you the society's child, the thing I hate more than most anything in life. Some days I get so mad at you for going to the water, for giving up before you died, for refusing the rafts the shop, your family, sent you past their own blood and error. Then, I remember that first quarter of psychology grad school a week before you died. When I was with Nona in Guthrie Hall, watching Lisa Schulman's seminar on healing the brain after loss, then needing to go to the bathroom to throw up. What did I do to you, dear boy, for telling you to suck it up? All my autodidactic bluster about African therapies and African coping mechanisms. All the chesty fables that I learned on Everett's knee in my self-created programs. All the newly-woke Nisqually hokum that I dumped on you. Who am I? God, who am I?

It is me who is making penance now, young brother, I tend bar and tend to the shop at a time when your loss fused the shop in ways I'm still trying to fathom. Eulalah took that grief and turned the shop building into a testing and vaccination site. We agreed to take a year off to rebuild and train our replacements. Losing you did take a step from her; she breathes a little harder than she used to, something she says is due to age but gets worse when the subject of you comes up. We keep it to good memories of you because if she thinks about it too deeply she spirals into despair.

Estelle left Scott the night she found out that you died, and divorced him six weeks later. She lives in the basement like she did when she was a teenager, helps out with the shop, and at night she works on a novel that will be an homage to your mother. She and Eulalah fuss like mother and daughter, and they really are mother and daughter now. Aisha still has the energy to balance both; she likes Seattle as much as she likes Tacoma (which is not much), but feels she has more places to hide when she's in school. They are an adorable mother-daughter team when they are in the shop together, but they are a little too steely to hear me say that too much.

Macalester is still here, tending to the door in case anarchists or anti-vaxx crazies show up. Macalester started taking Judith back and forth to the shop so she can be with people who care for her. She can't talk very much about you, or she gets into those same spirals, but I've seen an altar of you in her house. She still loves you, even in her silence.

As for Nona and me? We exchanged our vows last week. I don't know if this feeling is what you used to call "boyfriend/girlfriend island." I call it, "Happy Married Nigga Avenue," and I'm proud to call Aisha my stepdaughter. It seems that everyone outside of our circle thinks I'm such a disappointment and, to quote you, I could give less of a fuck. Though I am making only slightly less slinging drinks than I did as a counselor, people are very eager to tell me that I have lost my mind.

Yet the longer I have been away from being a counselor at Nisqually, the happier I've been. Scott Everett was the only father I have ever known. He worked with my aunt and mother to get me the scholarship to Nisqually and he stepped in after I lost them. He gave me structure, order, and a belief system that took away the pain I was feeling in my heart. I believed in Scott more than any man on earth, and I almost completely lost myself in that belief. I almost lost myself trying to salvage the good of that man. And the middle to upper-class kids who badger me about Everett when they recognize me fucking drive me insane. Again, I plead my culpability; I completely understand that some of these kids are dealing with public racial trauma and needed help handling it better, which was something I didn't give well. Most of them, however, are upper-middle-class Twitter thugs who call their big momma Betsy and their momma a bitch for not supporting their Venmo. I tried to reach all of them, and maybe I got to a few of them. Also, God knows Nisqually was due for some racial reckoning. However, I can't be a part of that atmosphere anymore. What I will do is make a different atmosphere: next month Nona and I are going back to grad school at UW Tacoma. And we are gonna have practice on the block, my brother.

We had a back-to-school party at the bar on my last shift; the entire shop plus Judith were there. The three hours we had were beautiful; we made it a private party, the Southern Kitchen catered, and my highlight of the night was when we taught Judith how to go through a *Soul Train* line. I was making sure everyone got in an Uber when Estelle started a rumination stupor, "you know, the first time I knew Scott was rotten was when I saw the best of him in mentoring you. I appreciated that he saw the traumas in your life and dedicated himself to making sure that your road was easier than his," she slumped down to sit on the curb, one leg sticking out into the road. "It was the best of him with you that convinced me that so much of what he was doing with us was bullshit." I sat down next to her and she put her head on my shoulder.

"When Vonetta left, he was the only person I could talk to. He was the only person who would talk to me. He told me he had lost his mother to drugs and that he could understand the pain I was going through. He was so vulnerable, and I thought I could heal myself by taking care of him in so much pain. Hell, I thought that through so much of our marriage. I edited so many of his articles and encouraged him to write more novels with the dream that their being in the world would help him become whole and grow. But it made him so incorrigible, so incorrigible." I didn't realize she was crying until I felt the tears soaking into my shirt. The Uber arrived and she lifted her head, wiping her eyes dry.

"You did well to move on with your life," she told me while getting to her feet. "You got a good job and the family, and you know this. I know Scott has got problems, but you got to understand something: you ain't one of 'em. The nigga got to put one foot in front of the other and move his Black ass on. I can't do what I did in the block and fix his problems." I opened the door for her and she slumped down into the back seat and Eulalah followed her in.

"That's for damn sure," said Eulalah.

I closed the door and wished them well, and sat down on the corner to meditate on all of it. Estelle, Scott, the shop, my mom, and you. My revelry was broken by seeing Scott across the block —for you and Aisha, I call him Scott now— shaking Kyle's pockets, herding him with side punches to cross to my side of the street as if he was cattle. Under the lights, I could recognize Darren and James trailing behind; one with a faded, torn multi-colored sweater, the other younger, with fatigues and a bald spot on his afro. Without hearing, I knew they were goading him for some money. Looking at Kyle, I started to get emotional about him, despite my best judgment. But the accumulation of seeing the boy being pushed around in such a feeble state got to me. Contrasting guilt and ire built in my stomach, mixing sourly with the alcohol. They metastasized with every interaction and harassment between them, and brought me to my feet when Darren and James started roughhousing him.

I rushed him and tried to push them off Kyle as a crowd came out of the other establishments. The two boys held me back while a group of men centered around Scott beating his son with a belt. Both young and old, the men were a mixture of exasperated and scared, trying to stop him from hitting his son and trying not to be hit. Behind them, a chair and bottle were surrounded by broken window glass.

"Stay the FUCK out of my business," Scott spat at me, "you are not a member of this family anymore. I am teaching this nigga some DISCIPLINE."

"You ain't doing shit, you evil nigga," said Kyle, stammering and trying to catch his breath. "I'm tired of your ass. I don't want to fuck with you no more. I don't want to fuck with you no more."

"You sloppy, lazy little bitch nigga. I'm gonna give you the goddamn ass whupping that I should have given you years ago, that your lazy heifer of a mother should have given you years ago." He snapped the belt in Kyle's direction to punctuate his point.

Outside the circle I could see Kevin Gregory, the owner of the bistro a block down from us, getting up from the ground. Then, on catching a glimpse of me, he ran over to rant at me, "I can't do this anymore," he said, "or at least I can't do it anymore with them. I try and be nice to them. I know they used to be artists and professors, but they hustle drinks from people every time they are here or try to buy bottles at discount prices. I can take the hit, but I can't take the fighting and breaking things."

"Call the cops and have them take them to jail."

Kevin hesitated, "I got a little crazy. I just waved a gun to get them out."

"Goddammit, Kevin."

"I'm sorry."

"This ain't the wild, wild west. You can't be doing this gunplay shit on a block where people are looking for excuses to ditch us."

The crowd started to get bigger, and I turned to see Aisha and Nona behind me. As Kyle was pouring snot and tears from his face, Scott twirled the belt he had in his hands in a circle.

"Jesus Christ, you niggas are stupid," said Nona, "this is a different fucking neighborhood now. You can't be doing the same fucked up nigga shit you used to. The cops are looking for reasons to clear your ass out, and you just gave them a million-dollar one."

Scott snapped the belt at Kyle again, and three bouncers came from the back to grab him and put him on the pavement. "I have tried and tried to help. I have tried to help this boy. I have tried to get him in touch with his best self, and what does this boy do to me? What does this soft-ass boy do to me?"

"I'm soft?" Kyle tried to rush his father, only to be grabbed by two people. "You ain't shit, you an evil nigga who abused my momma."

"Like you're one to talk, golf course Crip. We spoiled you, boy. We spoiled you. You were given everything, and you lived your goddamn life like a murderous brat. You never had a bad day in your life and turned out to be Mr. Golf Course Crip. And now I am going to teach you a lesson!"

"A lesson for what?"

"I try to help him," Scott said, pleading to the crowds and me. "I try to get him to get in touch with his best self. I try to get him to help us. I try and help him make us some money."

"Tell him what we were doing," said Kyle.

Scott looked at the crowd, silent, and stammered. "I am trying. No, I tried. I tried. You aren't my son anymore. You are no son of mine."

"Tell them what we were doing." Kyle was hovering over his father now, pinned down by two bouncers in black.

"I rebuke you. You are no longer my son," Scott spat up to him before trying once again to break free.

"You don't want to tell him? Then fine, I will. Do you want to know what I fucked up at?" Kyle turned to the crowd, "I fucked up at not making a beatbox for him. I was supposed to make beats so we can make money in your fake-ass rap label."

"You had the beats. You said you're a beat man. You're such a bougie son of a bitch that you couldn't make beats."

"I don't want to do that anymore. I want nothing to do with you. My mama don't talk to me anymore. I just want to go away from all this. I'm sick of your ass, I'm sick of your ass."

"Let him fight me. JUST LET him fight me. He wants to mess with me; I'll give him the ass whupping of his life. I'll give him the ass whupping he should have had for years."

"I'm tired of your ass. I don't want to mess with you anymore. I don't want to mess with you anymore."

And then, to use another parlance of yours, I lost my shit and grabbed Scott by the shoulders, lifting him half off the pavement, "look at yourself, motherfucker. Look at yourself! Almost thirty years ago, you came to me when this block was infested by old players and told me that there was a better way of life. That I didn't have to be that. That I could be a better Black man than a trap kid and that you could help me. And look at you right now, wearing a derby hat and beating your son, with two troubled overgrown little boys wearing camouflage."

"Fuck you, nigga," said Darren.

"We're going to kick your ass," said James, though neither made any motion toward me.

Scott held a hand up to simmer the two of them down, but they didn't pay him any mind. I dropped him back to the pavement and turned on them.

"You want to do it, then do it." I said. "But is that going to make your lives better? I remember when you two used to come to my office when you were in school, being so scared about succeeding in Nisqually. But look at you now. Look at you! Living off Scott's twos and fews, dreaming of making it in the rap game. Smelling like Hennessy and wearing dirty-ass fatigues." Scott struggled to his feet, and the bruisers around him put themselves on ready.

"And you," I said to Scott almost at the top of my lungs when I pushed him to the fence. "For all the crying you had about playas and hustlers in your entire life, you're the last hustler left, my nigga. Remember *Division Fork*, Nigga? Page 28: '*I had to survey a lay of the land to get home. If it wasn't for the police, it was the thugs and old playas who wanted something from me, and each day there and back was a different calculation.*'

"But look at you now" I said, as one of the bouncers put his hand on my shoulder, but didn't try to pull me away. "You the calculation, nigga. You the biggest thug on this block. You the nastiest playa left now. Everything you've touched you damaged or destroyed. You took the poison put upon you and put that poison on so many people. And it has to stop; it has to stop with me. I might fail, nigga, but at least I will fail honest. At least I will fail nobly. And least I will fail with my woman right with me. Remember the first sentence I ever told you: *I will do anything to get away from the players on these fucking blocks.*

I will do anything to get away from the players on these fucking blocks. Let me say this to you now, Scott... Playa, get the fuck out my motherfucking block."

I let him go and walked away, and the crowd started to disperse. "All right, boy," Scott said to Kyle, "time to go back to the apartment."

"Fuck you, dude. I followed you to hell. You were my daddy, and I followed you to hell. Followed you to hell." He let out an inaudible yell, ran into the middle of the road, and took a left into the darkness of an 11th and MLK side street.

"That's alright. That's alright," said Scott to the crowd surrounding us. "You don't know what I'm going to do. And you don't know how much you fucked up, Andre."

"Get the fuck off my block" I told him.

"You got too much of that respectable nigger shit in you. You don't know how the world will break you as a Black man, and you don't know the struggle that real niggas have had to go through."

"Get the fuck off my block."

He stabbed a finger at my face. "We could have done a lot of good shit. There's money on the table that you fucked up. We could have gotten some paper from Black Lives Matter in doing an abolition speaking tour. These White folks are going to republish my novel, and I'm getting to know people. I'm getting to know people!"

"Get. The fuck. Off. My Block."

Scott saw that no one was listening anymore, so he scooped up the belt and started walking away, but couldn't help turning back to try again. "And you're goddamn right I'm in a penthouse. I earned that shit, nigga. I earned it with the pain I had to go through at Nisqually. I earned it because niggas like you burned me. You. You. And you sitting here talking about me like I don't have all my pain! And that goes double for that bitch. What did the bitch do for me?"

And at the sound of the word bitch I lost it, I ran toward him and grabbed him by the throat. "Andre" Nona said grabbing my arm to get him off me "this ain't worth it."

"But this motherfucker" I said

"Nigga, I ain't doing this for him, get inside."

As I started to walk back while hyperventilating, Scott started screaming at the crowd already screaming at him. "She is talking about what I did and didn't do for her." I could hear him say above the uproar. "I took her ass out of the projects and made her respectable. And when I wanted her to do nothing but be the housewife like all the other White women, what did she do to me? The bitch got surly. The bitch didn't do anything for me when I needed her to be a woman and a wife."

"I'm a success," he said unabashed, in a higher-pitched voice than I ever heard him. "Everything good y'all book niggas have come from me! Every intellectual chance you got to compete with the White man come from me! Do you think you are doing something? I did something. I DID SOMETHING! I GAVE! I GAVE YOU NIGGAS A BLUEPRINT THAT YOU HAVEN'T LIVED UP TO! I gave so much to get out! I gave so much to mark my pain on that page! I gave so much to make it in the White world! And I just couldn't give anymore, motherfuckers! I just couldn't give anymore."

And as he said it, the crowd started to disperse. They had hollered at him at the top of their lungs a second ago, but as soon as he said that they stopped, they groaned, rolled their eyes, turned their backs and walked away. Scott kept screaming and screaming about how he couldn't give anymore until he was the only one left in the street. Looking at me inside the bar window, he began to open his mouth, fell silent, then walked to the other corner as I closed the drapes.

• • •

Dear Albert,

"The Hill" is a different place now, far different than you and I could have ever imagined it. Being away and bitter at first, I was agnostic about the subject of gentrification, hoping to be adrift among fellow hipsters. I didn't understand how money and cultural rivalries could turn my city into a tribal theme park. I've lost a good deal of my taste for internet outrage, Albert, but not completely. And the only thing worse than members of the Tacoma Police Department putting their knees on Manuel Ellis for thirteen minutes leading to his death was the gentrified members of the city who supported the cops who did it and voted for the politicians that enabled them. This doesn't mean the new group of Black Lives Matter members in the neighborhood help much either. That damn evil infomercial about the Blood who shot Corey Pittman on 15th Street broke my mind in half. Almost everyone I know my age on the block was traumatized by his loss, and now a bunch of cultural tourists and Twitter niggas are telling us that we bear some responsibility for that Blood blowing his head off randomly. And now babies are getting shot down again. Babies who, like Pittman, were just trying to go to school.

But I ain't leaving, dear boy. Remember that Arthur Miller play I told you to get that anti-Jew shit out of your head? Remember what one of the Kyle-ish sons said at the end of it, right before his momma started talking? Well, I'm not licked that easily, dawg, I'm gonna stay in my city and beat this racket. I'm gonna show outsiders and posers that you and the people who died here did not die in vain. You and so many others grew and fought your best out here and this is where I'm gonna win it for you. I'm gonna win it for you, for your mama, my mama, my auntie; for Mrs. Eulalah, Aunt Estelle, Nona, Aisha; and for Judith.

Why'd you do that, young nigga? It just seems like you are hiding, off the block, or in a bong funk somewhere. I keep expecting yo' ass to come back, say you're sorry, and tell me you're a dumb ass with a lot to learn. I search and I search and I can't understand shit about it. We are gonna have Judith's one-year sobriety party at y'all's house today. Today, my nigga. And you ain't home. You were free.

You were free, my nigga.

Rest well, my nigga.

I love you, my nigga.

Robert Lashley was a 2016 Jack Straw Fellow, Artist Trust Fellow, and a nominee for a *Stranger* Genius Award. His books include *Green River Valley* (Blue Cactus Press, 2021), *Up South* (Small Doggies Press, 2017), and *The Homeboy Songs* (Small Doggies Press, 2014). His poetry has appeared in *The Seattle Review of Books*, *NAILED*, *Poetry Northwest*, *McSweeney's*, and *The Cascadia Review*, among others. In 2019, *Entropy Magazine* named The Homeboy Songs one of the 25 essential books to come out of Seattle. *I Never Dreamed You'd Leave In Summer* is his first novel.